# WHAT MAKES
# A CHILD LUCKY

drawing by Fulvia Testa

# WHAT MAKES
# A CHILD LUCKY

## A NOVEL

❧

## Gioia Timpanelli

W. W. Norton & Company
*New York   London*

A portion of this novel originally appeared in *The Milk of Almonds: Italian American Women Writers on Food and Culture* by Louise DeSalvo and Edvige Giunta, eds. (Feminist Press, 2002).

For information about permission to reproduce selections from this book, write to Permissions, W. W. Norton & Company, Inc., 500 Fifth Avenue, New York, NY 10110

For information about special discounts for bulk purchases, please contact W. W. Norton Special Sales at specialsales@wwnorton.com or 800-233-4830

Manufacturing by Courier Westford
Book design by Rhea Braunstein
Production manager: Julia Druskin

Library of Congress Cataloging-in-Publication Data

Timpanelli, Gioia.
    What makes a child lucky : a novel / Gioia Timpanelli.—1st ed.
        p. cm.
    ISBN 978-0-393-06702-6
    1. Boys—Fiction. 2. Kidnapping—Fiction. 3. Survival skills—
Fiction. 4. Sicily (Italy)—Fiction. I. Title.
    PS3570.I463W47 2008
    813'.54—dc22

                                                    2008025045

W. W. Norton & Company, Inc.
500 Fifth Avenue, New York, N.Y. 10110
www.wwnorton.com

W. W. Norton & Company Ltd.
Castle House, 75/76 Wells Street, London W1T 3QT

1 2 3 4 5 6 7 8 9 0

For my parents, family, friends, the H.S., and *le Muse*, on whom so much in my life depends

For All Second Parents: Grandmothers, Grandfathers, Godparents, Aunts and Uncles, Teachers, Neighbors, and anyone else who has saved a child in the nick of time

For Giuseppina Milano and Vincenzo Timpanelli
&
Frances Morrison and Alphonse Timpanelli

With love and gratitude

# PROLOGUE

It is told again and again, there once was a father who had thirteen sons, and the youngest was called Tridicinu (Little Thirteen). This father didn't have any way to feed these children; he did the best he could, giving them soup to eat. The mother, to make them eat quickly, used to say: Whoever comes home first can eat a nice hot bowl of soup. Tridicinu was always the first home, so the hot minestra cotta was always his. But because of this luck, his brothers grew to hate him and planned a way to be rid of him. They sent him to the Ogres' house to bring back the Golden Bells, which the Ogres kept under their bed. Now, his brothers were sure that Tridicinu would never come back.

(The beginning of "Tridicinu," a Sicilian folktale)

# WHAT MAKES
# A CHILD LUCKY

For Nancy Willard

With appreciation
and affection,

Gibbons Ruark

pp. 26-27
"The Chestnut beds..."

# WHAT MAKES A CHILD LUCKY

Sicily at the end of the nineteenth century
or anyplace at anytime

"Hunger," she said, "is very personal. At first, it even tricks you into feeling guilty over your own misery, guilty for your human lack of grace. It holds your wrists tightly in its bony fingers; it breathes its foul breath into your gaping mouth as you sleep."

"But wait," we said, "doesn't this happen in a story Ovid tells about Erysicthon's hunger? What does it have to do with now? It's an old story."

"True, true," she said, "but why do you insist on being literal to time? You see, time might change the details, but the story of greed and retribution, or as you moderns insist of 'cause and effect,' is essentially the same. Erysicthon starves in his soul as well as his stomach. Why do you believe hunger could never happen to you, not where you are, and not now among your people? You think you are too well off for hunger to find you? Ah, my friends, we thought exactly the same."

# 1: NOW AND THEN
*(So much begins and ends with longing)*

❦

BECAUSE THIS land is flat and uninteresting it is barely noticeable, except in spring when a variety of wild greens appear in the fields. Some people around here think the Aunt and I are "innocents and idiots," to have opened the Inn where there are few roads and the possibility of even fewer guests.

"Well, we're off the main road and altogether beside the point," says the Aunt. It is true that hardly anyone comes here on purpose. Having gotten off the highway, most of our guests arrive hopelessly lost, so they are happy with a clean room and a hot meal. The Aunt likes "cooking by surprise" and I enjoy the company. We cook whatever we have in the pantry and it all works out.

"Arriving lost is a good way to come," the Aunt says,

and, because she especially loves chance meetings (calls them "fortuitous digressions"), she wants nothing to do with the clever person who comes for a purpose, doesn't trust anyone with even a small bur of a purpose at all.

"Those clever people can't fool me," she says. "I can spot a purpose from a hundred meters." Usually she is not given to extremes in thinking, but on this point she is adamant even when I tell her that I, too, first came here with a purpose. "No, no, my boy, that isn't the same. You came on the shabby heels of necessity. Necessity does not constitute a purpose."

But then what do we know of each other's lives? Even the most familiar shapes cast deep shadows. The Aunt calls the Inn "four cactus bushes and a falling-down stable." Sometimes when the moon plays games with the old place, it shows only a luminous and distinguished cabbage patch while the huge buildings fall into unrecognizable darkness. During the day, under the great sun of Sicily, which shines constantly on saint and thief alike, our shabby Inn looks like any other old farm building around here. Recently, we were told by the officials in the Ministry, who know these things, that the Inn has been judged "not suitable for profit."

"Just like us," says the Aunt, "just like us."

Since the best things can't be shown and the next best are often mistaken . . . we don't lament. Some say it's actually hard to find a "genuine place" anymore, and yet you will not find us in any of the new guides which threaten to expose with detailed maps the name and exact location of every small inn on the island; for this and every other graceful omission, the Aunt and I thank God.

I loved this land from the first time I chanced on it twenty or more years ago when I was a hungry boy searching the countryside for food to bring back to my family. Any abandoned place where I could filch a few greens and not get chased was a good place. That day I was mostly looking for cardoon, and it was at the edges of these fields that I found a good-sized plant. I cut some stalks and continued looking around until I found nice young ones. I knew all the work it took to get tough, old stalks ready to cook, so I was careful in my gathering. When I stopped I felt happy, not just because I had found the *carduna* but because I felt the fields themselves had welcomed me. Ah, you might not have liked the word "welcomed." You might have just thought, Fields can't welcome you. It's too romantic, pathetic fallacy and all that, yet places can and do welcome you. Of course, the opposite is true as well. I have been in fields that were ominous. Maybe terrible things happened there; I don't know. And then, of course, a hungry boy, a lonely donkey, a lovesick goat, a family of displaced mice, or a cunning weasel, might each have different standards for this reception.

On that day after I had a full bag, I stretched out (an unusual thing for me to do) and immediately I felt my body had found a perfect niche. I loved knowing that like every creature I, too, carried my bed with me and all I needed to do was lie down and it was made. I already had everything I needed; perhaps an exaggeration, but closer to the truth than its opposite. From that moment I knew that my life from beginning to end would be like this. All that I needed was to bring back what was already in my hands and I had my work and my bed.

"Are you complaining or bragging?" asked the Aunt when I read her what you just read.

"Neither," I answered, "it was just my way of telling my discovery and explaining my happiness."

"That's nice," she answered. "But when you say 'like every creature,' just remember, for whatever the reason humans carry more shadow space than any respectable donkey would need. The metric foot for this human shadow makes the land prices exorbitant. Talk about numbers close to infinity! Forgive me, Joseph, please tell what comes next."

It was a beautiful day. For a long while I followed a red bee buzzing in and out of a field of red clover, then closed my eyes and it was then that something else happened to me. I could feel, truly feel for the first time, the solid Earth moving. A great peace came with this motion and I slept. I don't know for how long, but when I awoke the deep blue sky was filled with giant clouds turning and slowly shifting, changing shapes. Beings and stories were everywhere. The celestial Cyclops were gathering their sheep into the moving caves, one, two, three of them; and when the clouds moved on, I picked up my bundle of stalks and moved on, too.

This place is not perfect, and I don't mean to have you believe that I thought it was. But where is perfect? Somewhere far away and grand, possibly Paris? I don't really know anything about Paris and I am not searching for any heavenly palazzo.

"Well, that's good," said the Aunt, "but I do wish you had written a little more about Paris."

My grandmother used to remind us children that the *kingdom of heaven is among you.* Yet most people like to travel to find interesting places to divert them—like beautiful mountains, the sea, or even volcanoes. Just last week a young couple came to the Inn, stayed three nights, and went off, just east of us, to climb a dangerously active volcano—an experience judicious people might want to avoid. At first, I thought it might be some kind of passionate pilgrimage in homage to Empedocles, but no, they were not the slightest bit interested in the old philosopher, his shoe, his story, or his metaphysics. They were, however, a pleasant and enthusiastic pair, so the Aunt and I enjoyed cooking for them. I last saw them at the train station, waving and smiling, eager to get to the mountain of ashes and hot stones for the privilege of possibly getting their backsides burned.

But then why should we imagine that we know any better than the beautiful moths? At night the Aunt and I make the rounds, carefully checking to see if all the shutters and doors are properly closed. We can't stand to watch some poor unfortunate creature reaching for heaven and then, *tzzip!*, sizzled by the bad luck of mistaking a lamp for the real thing, not that I could tell you for certain what the real thing is, but if moths can be fooled, then we had all better watch out.

The second time I came back to these fields involved evil, a word sensible people try not to say aloud. I've seen people shrink when they hear it, and like everyone else I was taught to avoid it. *Don't stare evil in the face, for it will take notice and turn toward you.*

My mother said, "Don't ever get involved with bad people and situations. If, God forbid, you find yourself in a bad thing, try to right it if you can, without causing more trouble, and then, Sons, turn on your heels, shudder, and thank the Blessed Mother of Tindari for getting you out of there with your skin," but I did get caught by evil, and although I escaped with my life, for a while it held

a good portion of my young skin in its fist. Then something strange happened. When evil turned its attention
elsewhere, right in front of me misery dropped something
of real value, and without thinking, I scooped it up on the
run and put it into my pocket.

This is the story of my thirteenth year when everything changed for me, once and forever. I remember a
teacher saying, *Follow your destiny,* which is a hard counsel
for people to trust, but I have always taken to it as though
I had no willful choice in the matter. Where I am short-
sighted, nature sees cycles and possibilities.

So this is the story of that time, but don't ask the Aunt
for her story. "What story?" she would say. Yesterday, she
asked, "What's left in the pantry?"

"Lentils," I reported.

"Lentils? Good, that's my story for today. We'll break
some spare pasta and make a thick lentil soup."

We spent a good amount of time sorting out the
debris from the mound of lentils on the table and into old
pots on our laps, no talking, just calm patience. The story
yesterday was a very good *minestra,* with no tiny stones,
sticks, or earth in it. A good winter story of how we got
the lentils, prepared them, cooked them, and what happened after that.

The best things are not easily seen or explained, the next
best are misunderstood, and the rest is up for speculation,

good conversation, or at least a small written story. Anyone or anything that is needed the Aunt searches out or waits for, but don't ask for her story, she won't tell it.

"You're the storyteller, Joseph," she encourages. "You tell what happened with you and the bandits."

I love the old tales. Growing up I heard my great-grandmother tell them on winter nights. We children laughed a lot while we learned about giants, beings we already felt but now had a name for. I can hear a friend complain, "There are NO giants, hasn't anyone told you yet?" Ah! True enough, but what other name do you call that huge unthinking gross being that took away your breath and delicate ways of thinking while it marched hungry, very very very hungry, and settled into your neighborhood, eating everything you loved? On the good side, the stories of giants always told what very ancient treasures the giants have stored that we can take or are given to us. We heard and loved stories about knights and giants, cruel kings and kind ones, queens, benevolent or otherwise, and of course Ogres. My town was big on a family of Ogres that my brothers and I believed were really living in the town garbage dump, a respected and fearsome place. My father's laughter and explanation to the contrary could not convince us.

Next, there were the daily stories, *histories*, my father called them. *What happened to Ziu Turiddu when he went to*

*Messina? What did La Nanna Angelina do to help Grandpa's atelier finish the opera house in Palermo?*

In one way or another my parents told stories about everything, so that even if you hadn't known your great-great-grandparents or if the part of town they lived in had changed (not likely in those days), you could still "see" the places, actually "see" them by hearing the stories. Everything was familiar, even the ordinary tragedy of our lives were in those stories. The stories stayed the same, while we changed in them, so a story you heard at five was one thing, at eight another, and now at thirty another, and so on. You could measure how much you changed and understood by what you were hearing and imagining in the stories.

My parents' own story was a little particular. (The Aunt has just guffawed at my understatement.) My mother came from country people who tilled a small piece of land on a nobleman's estate. "Life was always poor, difficult, unfair," she said, "but we were dignified, honorable, filled with respect and love, and we never lacked for something good to eat." My father's people, teachers and scholars, lived in town and faced neither bed nor table with dread. My parents fell in love at a harvest supper and they never looked back. They were not encouraged by their families. My Uncle Michele wrote a famous family letter to my father, *This "in love" business causes a great deal of trouble in the neighborhood, but it is something we Sicilians cannot*

*avoid, no matter how many institutions they put in our way.*
*What can I say,* figliu miu, *what can I say?* Despite terrible
arguments in my mother's family and terrible silence in
my father's, my parents did manage to marry.

Like both his parents (in his family women were tra-
ditionally educated as teachers of Greek and Latin), my
father inherited a love of scholarship and teaching, but in
this and in other things my father was not lucky. Because
of a certain family tragedy, consequential and finally fatal,
my father never realized his youthful plans or dreams, but
since that is another story, I will let the buzzing memory
go. But, I repeat myself, my father, in terms of the world,
was not lucky, but as for love the reverse was true.

We were born about ten kilometers from here in my
parents' town, where we all finally returned after having
twice traveled the Island following my father's work. At
that time, he was an amanuensis for composers and nota-
ries. We went with him because my parents would not be
separated.

"*Madness,*" said both sides of the family, for it was
unthinkable then that because of a man's work the whole
family should be displaced. Usually if a man could not find
work near home, his wife and children stayed safely in the
family house, where they had a roof over their heads and
grandparents to help and family and neighbors and friends
who knew them well. Of course, this old way made sense.

In those days, there was no work to be found in or around our town. The men had to travel back and forth to huge farms, sometimes coming home only twice a month, but my parents refused this unsatisfactory arrangement, so we left our town. "Where are you going?" we were asked by my paternal grandfather, more than once. Once we lived in a caravan, left us by a family of Gypsies who had befriended my father. We stayed in that caravan for eight blissful months. My mother sang all the time and my father and brothers walked to Palermo, where he worked for a famous librettist. But the following year all his work ended and hunger came again, and in the city it was far worse than in our own town. We finally packed up what we had and went back to live in our great-grand-mother's house.

By the time I was nine my parents were struggling to survive, and yet because I was born with a caul my mother always said she had no fear for me even though I was the last boy and the smallest. At my birth an old man told her that this birth "cover" would bring me luck, or to say it differently, that things, even the most ominous, would turn out in my favor. It was a sign. I would be a lucky child.

"Superstition, sympathetic magic, not verifiable science, not even good poetry," my father said, "but I see the way you are. There is something in your nature, my boy, that invites luck."

"What's that, Father?"

"I couldn't tell you exactly, or I'd give it away in a bottle or at least write about it. And I know that you are more curious than frightened. *Hic sunt leones.*"

"But I am afraid of lions," I said.

"Good, there is a trait that will make you lucky."

We both laughed and never talked about cauls or my possible "luck" again. I took what he said as fair, for although lavish with his affections, my father was careful with his words, and he complimented my brothers when they merited it, always finding the most appealing and affectionate words to describe those he loved.

Before I was nine, I was working around town, helping people as they needed, and bringing home some bread that way. In the evenings, our father continued to teach us to read and write. We all loved to hear him read from his precious books and I secretly hoped to be given the chance to finish the work of translation on an old text that he and his sister had begun, something none of my brothers had the slightest desire to do. And so we lived together in the abandoned beauty of my father's life and in the brave and courageous caring of my mother's.

Our house was small and what people now call "dilapidated," for we had to make "adjustments" to do the simplest things: use a chair to prop open a door, move another one to keep the door closed. Put a flat stone under the table leg to even it, get a stick to keep a window open. In short, everything had something else to keep it closed, opened, or upright. If the house was a foundering vessel, the bed we three youngest slept in was already derelict. I just remembered that my father called our house the Wreck of the Medusa.

At night, before we climbed into that magnificent, listing ship, we all gathered around it to say a child's prayer, taught to us by our Great-Aunt Rosaria.

*Iu mi cuccu di stu littu,*
*Cu Maria supra pittu . . .*
*Iu dormu, Idda sviglia*
*Si c'è cosa, mi sdruviglia*
*Mi cuppuna cu So mantu*
*In nome Del Padre, Figliu, e Spiritu Santu*

*(I sleep in this bed, with Mary o'er my breast; if something happens she will wake me; she covers me with her mantle; in the name of the Father, Son, and Holy Spirit.)*

The chestnut bed had been my great-grandmother's. It was beautifully carved with delicate branches of lemon leaves (you could sometimes smell their fragrance), in whose dense center were the face and wings of an exquisitely carved angel. Its strongly lined grain was polished and I loved its feet, which were carved lion's paws. This great bed took up the entire corner of our one room, but I imagined it in my grandparents' huge bedroom. By the time we slept in it the feet had lost toes and one foot had run off altogether, half the mattress ropes were missing, and the mattress itself needed refilling, which kept it sagging whether any of us slight boys were in it or not. Even as a child, I thought of its beauty and its precarious state as one and the same. The world came to me not only in the rich wood and beautifully carvings, but also in its listing and standing straight. To not tell you of the look of the bed, complete with its falling and standing, would be to deny the spirit that was inside my life, although what exactly that spirit was I could not say, not then, not now.

We all know that some years are leaner than others, but when I was twelve we, along with our neighbors, had slipped into a terrible poverty. My father now walked with the other men as a day laborer in another part of the province and came home every third day, until that place no longer had work for them and they all came home to stay. Although my parents worked as hard as they could, they often did not have enough to feed us. That year I remember noticing the smell of hunger. Yes, hunger has a smell, both sweet and acrid at the same time—like some food gone bad. Hunger is a funny thing, for it is personal, even intimate. If you've never been hungry you never think it could happen to you, certainly not where you are, but it is so intimate that when it happens it happens only to you and only where you are. It searches you out and becomes the roof over your head, the floor beneath your feet.

Once you have lived through this you cannot let any starving person or creature that you meet go away hungry. Although some days we didn't have a slice of bread, each day my mother made a big pot of soup, one day chicory, another day escarole, another day *brocculiddi*, another day onions, whatever she could manage or find. (It was at this time I became good at collecting wild greens.) It was right that we all shared this one pot of soup, but we were never full. Like all creatures we lived day by day, but whatever the hour we were always hungry. At that time, my poor father was too ashamed or dejected to read to us and all reading and writing stopped, no matter how hard my mother urged us to keep on as before. After saying our prayers at night, we went to bed hungry and disheartened. *We were down to our fingers and sucking our teeth.*

Then one night after my parents fell asleep my older brothers made up a little game—whoever got home first at dinnertime would be the one to eat a full bowl of hot soup my mother had simmering on the back of the stove. Since my mother and father were out working, they would not see this game. My big brothers were so sure it would be one of them to eat the whole bowl that they made bets with each other. When we younger boys, excited about the chance, whispered our secret hopes to each other at night, they laughed at us, but an unexpected thing happened. On the first day, I was first; on the second day, I was first; on the third day, I was again first; and then I was first on every day after that. My brothers were surprised as they ran in from their work right behind me, but no one could beat me. I don't know how it happened that the last and littlest was the first, yet each day I won—and sure enough, I would have that nice full bowl. But because I won, a thin crack was made in the bowl of our old life and unhealthy and mysterious stains were growing along that crack.

In the end this little game changed our lives. My brothers, who had always loved me, or at worst been indifferent to us little ones, now became annoyed and then angry. What could I do? Was it my fault that I couldn't lose? When they stopped talking to me, I couldn't believe it, and tried forcing them to be friends with me again, but they pushed me away. Finally, when they couldn't even look at me, I knew beyond a doubt that they hated me, really hated me. I was no longer one of them.

Of course, as I first said my parents were not at home to see this. My mother, who had been working for a woman at the other end of town, came home unexpectedly one day, saw and understood the game, and stopped it. I can still see her trembling hands as she got out the bowls and divided the amount equally, then she carefully put in a piece of bread from the half round she had carried in, sat down in her chair, buried her head in her hands, and cried. I went to comfort her and to ask for forgiveness, but she shook her head saying, "It's not your fault, my boy, you are not to blame. You children are not to blame." But it was too late. There was no doubt I had stepped out of my brothers' circle—I was now an outsider, something I could never have even imagined before.

Naturally, this little story of my coming home first each day was told around by the children and from that time on people in town called me Lucky, which in our town also meant "La Fortuna Nera," bad luck. Irony is never lost on my people, but you have to be careful neither to ignore bad luck (you might get taken up in a grand way) nor to court it (you might wake up married to it!). So Lucky is what they called me, but it was not a name I liked or would have called myself. I laughed at the name.

I would never have thought of Lucky as my name. I would have called myself the Fix-it Kid. People were always calling on me to fix things. That's what I really was, a fixer of anything. I was always fixing pots, buckets, chairs for our family and our neighbors, and finally, one Sunday, that beautifully carved, lopsided bed. But no one ever gets to give themselves a nickname. "Lucky," they said, "you must be the fastest runner of all those boys." But, you know, I wasn't. Or sometimes they'd say, "You must have a strong will!" But really my older brothers had the greater desire to be first. Some people even said, "Ah! Someone is looking after you," I didn't ever think about that, either, but one thing was clear to me—that because of this "good fortune" my brothers had thrown me out and there was nothing my parents could say or do to get me back into their good graces.

At this time, I made a great friend, a wine merchant named Pasquale. He was a courageous, open hearted man of twenty whom everyone in town loved and respected. I had once fixed his cart and once given his donkey some cool water out of my *quatarella,* which he never stopped thanking me for. Even my father, a playful observer of people, said Pasquale was a special soul. In our town they told the story that at fifteen he had saved an entire family from murderous bandits. I adored him as only a kid can. I started going to his mother's wine shop to help them whenever they needed me. At this time I was still a little snotty-nosed *muccarusu,* yet he talked to me the way grown-ups talk to each other—as an equal. He used to say, "Kid, you work as hard as any man in town—harder, because you measure things correctly." That he talked to me like this gave me heart, especially at that time.

Pasquale would often go to Vittoria, a town in our province famous for its wine, and with his donkey, Artù, bring back a cartload of wine for the shop. Before he went this one time, I asked him if he was afraid of the bandits that everyone in town said had come back to our neighborhood. He laughed and said, "No," and then he showed me the gun he carried. He even let me hold it. It was heavier than I had thought. I let out a curse word, long and loud, the first I ever uttered in front of a grown-up. He hesitated and then laughed. I laughed, too, and handed him back the gun, which was also much colder than I had imagined.

The trouble concerning the bandits began slowly the year before. They would appear in a district, rob some poor traveler, and then hide for months until one day they struck again, leaving behind a recurring nausea of fear. The state authorities had been called in to find them, but the gang had eluded the *carabinieri* so far. Although we had a coach that twice a day went back and forth between our town and the provincial capital with no incidents, honest people who had to travel out into the honest countryside began to consider the public roads no-man's land. Everybody in town talked in hushed tones about these bandits, everyone except Pasquale.

"Will you help me with the demijohns tomorrow?" he asked one day.

"Sure, I'll be there. Do you need help going to Vittoria?"

"No." He smiled. "I can do this alone, Kid. Don't push your luck."

I accompanied him out of the town square, where we passed a hunter coming in from the countryside carrying a string of limp and lifeless songbirds, carelessly flung over his shoulder. I almost said something to Pasquale, but then thought better of it. It felt like an omen.

"I'll see you tomorrow morning," he said as he went out the town gate.

That afternoon by three o'clock our Sicilian sun was burning close, the sky like the sea, deep, deep blue, beautiful, never-ending. The town was quiet. It was siesta and almost everybody was asleep, keeping this *l'otta di lu caudu*, time of heat. I got out of bed and, half dreaming, went to sit outside on the steps, leaning my head against the cool wall, when I heard shouts coming from the square. In the square two men on horseback, leading a donkey, were shouting something I could not understand. My father came out. "What is it?" he asked me. Then my mother came out making the sign of the cross. "What's happened? What's happened?" Then, one by one, we understood what the men were shouting,

"They've murdered Cumpari Pasquale. They've murdered Cumpari Pasquale." Over and over they shouted, "They've murdered Cumpari Pasquale."

More and more people started to appear in the square,

leaving their houses like sleepwalkers, and as the crowd grew, so did the lament: men and women and children followed the body, all of them crying. This terrible procession grew in number, wailing as it went around the winding street to finally stop at Pasquale's house. And when his mother, father, brother, sisters, and when finally Mariuzza, his little pregnant wife, came out, everyone fell silent. It was as though the whole town's heart broke then and there. His mother screamed the most terrible sound I've ever heard and the little wife fainted. In the confusion I went up to the covered body slung over the saddle. I kept hoping it wasn't him, maybe it was someone else, a stranger, a mistake—but it was him, it was Pasquale; I could tell by the place where his shoe was torn.

# 2: HOW I GOT INTO TROUBLE

### ❧

Eventually the town pieced together a story. Pasquale had bought a full cartload of wine in Vittoria (that was so) and had turned onto the major road coming back into our town when the highwaymen stopped him. People said there must have been some exchange of gunfire and that the bandits fled (no one knows that for certain), making Pasquale feel safe enough (he never thought such a thing) to continue onto a narrow road that led to a shortcut. One of the bandits, who must have known this mountain path (a betrayal?), waited for him to pass and shot him in the back, taking the donkey and cart to the others on the road. What exchanges humans make!

Pasquale's death brought me tremendous grief, a

weight that I had never carried before. Without him the life I had been living came to an end. I was inconsolable. There was no one as wonderful as Pasquale, people said again and again. He was forthright, honorable, just, and kind. Oh, we all moaned for him, for his family, for ourselves. All his friends talked again about their own lack of virtues. Why was there such injustice in the world, that the very best are murdered? Once such a thing happens, the inevitable fall of cards comes down on the table. Pasquale's death created a series of unexpected events that arranged themselves to include me.

The next morning, my older brothers told me that the Mayor of our town wanted to see me right away, within the hour. What did such an important man like the Mayor want with a kid like me? Perhaps it was my silly pride, but because my brothers were paying attention to me and wanted me to do something for them, I fell into this story, believe me, unwittingly. It all happened so fast that I didn't get a chance to reflect or even to tell my mother, who was sitting with the little widow. My older brothers took me to Town Hall. I was happy until I saw their stupid nudges and conspiratorial laughs and could not interpret these as love. They left me at the threshold of the huge Municipal Building, rang the bell, and ran away.

Although I knew the Town Hall, I had never been inside. It was the place for mysterious and high-and-mighty agreements and such. To me it looked like a big palace, and like every building in our town the rooms were mostly bare, with the exception of a few pieces of huge furniture that were broken or badly fixed. The place overwhelmed me, but I was not fooled by the Mayor himself. Pasquale had never liked him. Once he told me, "He's the kind of man who wants to give you the impression that he has nothing on his mind, nothing to hide, nothing urgent he wants from you. But don't you believe it, Kid." I thought of this as I stood in front of him with my cap in my hands. He was yellow like tallow, with a round, baby, epicene face. Everything about him made you think he was harmless. He got things done, he always said, only by arranging them, "arranging a little here, arranging a little there, nothing big." That's what he said, but don't you believe it.

"Come, come, my boy, sit down," he said in that high-pitched, accommodating voice of his. "Sit, sit. Your brothers have given you the highest recommendation for a simple job I need done." I sank into the large stuffed chair, and pieces of lumpy horsehair stuffing poked me here and there. My first experience with greatness was not comfortable.

"There are some newly arrived craftsmen in our area," he said, waving his hand in a spiral above his head. (In our town that gesture shows how important they are, as if they were some kind of nobility.)

"Craftsmen? What craftsmen?" I said as I noticed one of the drawers was missing from the grand credenza and in another place a knot in the wood had fallen out, leaving a gaping hole. Imagine making a beautiful piece of furniture like that and then using a board with such a deep tree knot in the front. It is a terrible thing about my mind: while experiencing extraordinary moments it goes on seeing the world in its ordinary cracked way.

"Well," he continued, "these craftsmen, these important strangers, are needed to work on the Town Hall, and we need you to bring a message to them, saying we would like to hire them. It's as easy as that."

"Listen, Your Honor, why give this job to strangers, what about my brothers and me? We could do any fixing jobs you might have." He looked at me for a second and then laughed hard and long, as though he had a case of high-pitched hiccups. After a little "Heh, heh," I protested, saying I couldn't go anywhere to find strangers, my family wouldn't allow it, but he ignored me as though I hadn't said anything. All the while I kept trying to get out of that terrible stuffed chair, but he kept pushing me back down, and with each push that awful smile of his grew larger. Then he went to his desk and picked up a single sheet of paper. I took the opportunity to get out of the chair, hoping to run out as fast as I could when his back was turned.

"Stop where you are! Ah! I see you are in a hurry to

execute your duties, official duties. These duties, you know, cannot be questioned, since you are, after all, a soldier in our charge—and you know what happens to soldiers who desert," he said, looking into the distance with a little wistful smile. Then, taking the piece of paper, he ceremoniously put it in a leather sack. "If you don't do this and do it well, the consequences will be serious for you and your family. Here, put this safely on your belt and take great care of it. You see how many seals there are to protect it from the wrong eyes?" I took the leather sack, and that was that. I was a little embarrassed to have him see that my belt was only a piece of rope as I slipped the sack onto it with a knot.

"There! Don't make things complicated for yourself. You're a simple messenger," he said, making a joke. "Or rather, you are an official messenger, do you like that better? You are a smart boy, and they say a lucky boy. Now you will have a chance to prove both, eh? This is why you have been chosen, a boy sure of himself." He gave me directions where to find the strangers. "Now be a goat and climb with feet as sure as a goat." He put his arm around my waist and pushed me to the door. "Come back to me soon," he said, giving me a big smile with those ugly yellow teeth of his. So my brothers had sent me to hell and as I ran down the hall I wondered what it would take to get me out of there.

I left the building dazed; everything looked strange to me and for a minute I didn't know where I was. My three oldest brothers were peeking around the corner. "I'm here," I said, then I called out their names. They walked away from me quickly and then broke out into a run. I didn't call their names twice; instead I turned, and never looked back.

I put my cap on and immediately whistled a song I used to sing all the time.

*Truvau' un capidduzzu, ch'è tantu sapuritu,*
*Quanu me l'aggia' metteri?*
*Quanu mi fazzu zittu*

*Zitti cun i pompi*
*Zitti cun i banieri*
*Tutti ca me chiamano*
*Buon Giornu, Cavalieri*
*Ti ri Tiri ddi ti*
*Ti tì*

It's a song about a boy who finds a "good, sweet hat," which he plans to wear as a bridegroom. He thinks, "Ah! I'll put feathers in it," and that gets him to imagine flags and pompons, and soon he's a beautiful knight, "*un cavalleri.*" Look at what finding a hat does! Well, there is no lack of imagination in my town. I laughed out loud and kept whistling.

I knew I was in trouble. Although I didn't know exactly what this was all about (that was to my advantage), I knew I was being sent on a bad mission. Not wanting to explain or get my family involved, I didn't even go home but went instead to the road out of town. The Mayor had said these men would pay me something for my trouble, men who were staying in this old farmhouse in a section of the mountains he described, a place one could not even get to with a donkey and cart anymore but only on foot, ever since a landslide had blocked an old pass. It was above the fields where I had picked the cardoon, near a place that was known as the Cat Boulders. If I was right, it was also the abandoned farmhouse where I had gathered chestnuts as a present for my mother. It was a strange coincidence. I knew the ruin well. It had once been my secret place.

I figured I would do the best thing for myself: find a borderline where they would not yet know that someone was coming, a place that they did not watch or consider theirs, where I could hide on my side and watch for them. If I could find the right spot, I'd sit patiently, wait for them to leave, hang the Mayor's message on their door, maybe even look around, and then beat it. The only trouble with this plan was that I knew these borderline places were not usually obvious.

I got to the mountain road, and after a two-hour climb I found the Cat Boulders. In ten minutes the footpath ended, but I kept walking. The sun was hot, and after a while I realized I had been walking for a long time and still hadn't found the place to turn. Then I saw the land was changing, and I was getting to a high spot where the chestnut trees would be and, sure enough, there before me was the clearing I remembered, but all I saw was a heap of rubble, dust, and fallen rocks from what must have been the old farmhouse. There was hardly any green left around the ruins. No orchard. Nothing. All the chestnut trees, except one, had been cut down or had died. Finally, I walked slowly to the one huge chestnut, all the while looking around, but I neither saw nor heard anyone—I had found my hiding place—I almost rejoiced as I crouched down behind it. I could smell the bark, very dark with wide deep ridges. I remember running my hand over it, like touching a friend on the shoulder for no reason except to be noticed. I watched a tiny, almost diaphanous spider making a web between the rough ridges of bark while a line of serious ants marched in single file up the tree on the very next ridge. I was feeling too safe.

I should have remembered my mother's saying, *Cu vidi chiu di lu padrunu, e urvu,* who sees more than the owner is blind, because just as I was congratulating myself for having found this perfect hiding place something moved not twenty feet from my head. A woman, who must have been standing there perfectly still for as long as I had been in the clearing walked right up to the tree and stared down at me.

"Get up!" she said. "What are you doing here?"

"I'm just carrying a message to some workmen," I said, feeling like a real fool. "I was told by their friend the Mayor that they might be living here. Maybe I could just give Thee the message, Signora, and then go home," I added feebly.

"What are you talking about? Are you crazy? Go back home? Now that you're here you can't just go back," she said. "In the first place, how did you know to come here? And what 'friend' of yours sent you to these 'workmen'?" she laughed. Not expecting an answer, she told me to follow her. It was then that I noticed she had a pistol in her left hand. As she walked, it moved in and out of the folds of her skirt. I had found the place, all right.

When we got to the pile of stones, she opened a door that I hadn't noticed before and I could see that the farmhouse, although in ruins, was still on its feet, or rather on its knees. The place was no more than a hovel. It was dark and hot, and on the stove something was cooking. It smelled great. I stood there thinking, Boy, this dump smells like heaven.

"What are you doing?" she asked.

"Nothing, I'm just standing here," I said.

"What you mean, you're just standing there? You're not just standing there, you're smelling the air like a fox. Do you want some of those chickpeas?"

"Yes, I wouldn't mind tasting a little, thanks," I said, a bit too eagerly. She brought me a small pot of chickpeas in one hand and a huge spoon held by her thumb against the most falling-apart chair in the other. I took the pot and sat down carefully on the almost nonexistent raffia seat; and right there in the middle of the room dove in with the big spoon. The chickpeas were good, too, the taste of the cooked onions was so sweet. But before I could take another mouthful she returned from the stove shouting, "Wait a minute," as she made a thin cross with some oil over the chickpeas. "Wait a minute," she said again, as she ground black pepper over it. "Wait a minute," she growled, as she handed me a slice of bread from her pocket. "Now it's just about right and you can eat!" Well, Thank God, I thought. I hadn't eaten, not even a piece of old bread, since the day before, unless you count the cactus pear I had picked on the way out of town. On this score things were looking up.

Night—and still no one came. After the chickpeas, she and I hardly said four words together. Since the chair was about to fall apart I went to sit on a sound bench against the wall. As far as I could see, it was the only thing that wasn't sick unto death and in need of some emergency attention. I was so tired that I fell asleep sitting up against the cold wall.

"What are you doing?" she shouted, shaking me hard.

"I'm sleeping," I answered, standing up, not wanting to be disrespectful.

"At a time like this you're sleeping? Are you *babbu e fissu* for real or just crazy?"

"No," I said, not liking to be called such a stupid and impotent a thing as *babbu e fissu*. "No, I'm just tired. I always sleep when I'm tired," I explained.

She shook her bristly dog-hair head and gave me that look that only old people can give you when they're assessing your possible future, or, in this case, lack of one. She walked away; I fell asleep immediately and didn't remember anything until the door opened and I heard her deep voice.

"Don't be so fast to kill this kid, he has some message for you, and besides, look at him, he's only a baby."

"Yeah! Yeah! Baby, my ass. When the *carabinieri* come to kill us, what'll you call him then? Where's this message?"

She shook me and I got up. I stood there facing four men, the highwaymen who had just come into our countryside and were certainly the murderers of Pasquale. I was absolutely sure. When I realized I was staring at them, I looked down. I could see they would not think twice about killing me, for they had no natural human connection to me, and although they looked at me hard, I knew they did not see me. The Boss had the most glassy, dead eyes I had ever seen. It was these eyes that really struck me. They had no visible soul cord behind them. My Mother called it the string that connects the heart to the eyes: *You can always see this string by looking into people's eyes.* His string had slipped, his heart had probably been wrenched a long time ago, and his good soul was now way out of reach, way out. I hung my head.

"Look at me, you fool. Where's this message?" he asked quietly, all the while looking at the bag. I quickly slipped the knot and gave it to him. Only one of them could read, and he walked outside with the Boss and the others. They left me in the house with the woman. She stood shaking her head again as if to tell me I had already made enough mistakes, but I smiled, shrugged, and sat down on the bench again, looking around for windows and doors, which now I could distinguish from the general rubble. Although I knew that an offering of chickpeas was not necessarily a sign of complete undying loyalty to a stranger, it just might be something, but I couldn't count on it. After a while they came back and gave me a package to give the Mayor and said I was to return to them with the answer before noon of the next day. If not, they would come to town, find me, and kill me on the spot. This glorious messenger business was getting to be monotonous and dangerous.

"Don't think I only mean you, my boy. Isn't your father the son of the failed schoolteacher from Bellafranca? Do you understand? I know you. You must be a smart kid if you're working for the Mayor."

"Or a real moron," one of them added under his breath.

I knew that I was what they considered "a real moron," you know, an innocent who gets mixed up in a terrible mess by chance. I was caught, caught fast, and had put my family in danger.

"I understand," I answered. "I work for the Mayor as his official messenger." When I said the word "official," I smirked, which was something I had just learned from them. They liked this humor and laughed. I had to be careful not to be too smart, because without even thinking I can be a mimic. I don't even mean to do it, it just comes over me and there I am sounding like the person who's talking to me. Those days it ran riot over me, and I had as much choice as a tamed parrot. They liked the stupid humor and didn't think I would be mimicking them. After all, what person in his right mind would do that?

Then one of them, a small man with a deep scar that

went from his forehead to under his eye, looked at me. I looked back and saw that one of his eyes was closed. It was scarred and the other was squinty. I turned my head and he came up to me, stroked my cheek, and said, "Ah! that's what we like—a clever boy, as long as he isn't one of those stupid fools who thinks his tongue is clever, too." I stepped back and almost spit at him but didn't. The others were deadly silent. The old woman moved and every eye was on her.

She faced the Boss. "Did you hear me?" she asked under her breath.

"I heard you, but did this smart aleck understand? Who can ever tell what the Crazy One will do?" Everyone laughed. Well, so they didn't like clever kids and the guy with the eye was called the Crazy One and the old woman had some influence, but who knew how much? I took the package without a word and walked out of there. They laughed at me again, but I kept walking. Once I got on the right road back to town I kept feeling eyes watching me, and maybe they were. The package burned in my hand. What was in it? What had the Mayor wanted of them? Of course, I thought of money right away, but somehow it didn't feel heavy enough, and yet it was heavy, but not compact like money. Whatever it was, I could smell that it was wrapped in some badly cured leather. I thought of just getting off the road and opening the damned thing to see what was in it. But really I had no plan. I wondered what

clever thing my brothers had told my parents, and then I
thought of a story that an old uncle in our town used to
tell about a boy who was sent by his brothers, who didn't
like him, to get the Golden Bells from the Ogres' house.
No one expected this boy to get back. Here I was leaving
the Ogres' den and all I could think about were the Bells.
Where were the Bells?

Soon I was back in town and in the Mayor's office
without anyone stopping to talk to me. Kids are never
invisible in my town, so it was surprising I hadn't come
across anyone who saw me before getting to the Town
Hall, but no one did. It was a little piece of luck.

"Well, well, you're back already, are you? What have
you got for me?" The Mayor took the package. "Did they
give you anything?" I knew he meant money.

"No, but that's fine," I said. I didn't like to think I was
really his messenger, or theirs, either.

"Here," he said, flipping me a piece of real silver.

You owe me a few more pieces, I thought, but took it
anyway.

"Come back tomorrow morning at seven-thirty," he
said. "I'll have an answer for them. Be sure you say nothing
of this. People would be jealous of outsiders working here."

"Sure," I said, "don't worry."

"Worry?" he answered. "I wouldn't think of it, nor
should you," and he flashed that yellow canine smile of his.

I flashed a smile back, not to be outdone, and backed out of the room bowing with my hand clutching my stomach in a mock courtier's gesture. I ran down the stairs and slammed the front door after me. And when I was out on the street I heard a loud chain of curse words from the Mayor's open window. Whatever was in the package, the Mayor hadn't liked it.

Next, I went to Pasquale's wake and tried to say a prayer at the coffin, but I couldn't seem to get the words right—Pasquale lying there in his coffin looked more like his grandfather than himself. He looked about a hundred years old. When I went to pay my respects to his wife Mariuzza, with her little gray face, sitting like a stone beside the body, I put the silver coin in her small hand without anybody seeing me. It seemed to get her out of a trance and she clutched my hand and wept. I put my arm around her little shoulders to steady her while she wept and wept uncontrollably on my hand. We stood a long time like that, crying.

Her sister-in-law came and helped her sit down again. I turned to the line of mourners at the wall and found an empty chair and sat down next to some men who were talking about what had happened. I recognized Pasquale's Cousin with his two boys. They used to live outside of our town on a farm they owned (they were almost *borghesi*), but now they lived in a town on the other side of Enna.

He was talking about a gang of bandits who had recently terrorized a baronnessa and her nephews. The Cousin was in the middle of the story.

"They knew that on August twentieth the Baroness Cinciano received the rents. The next morning her nephew—do you know Baron Spandolieri?—well, he and his young son Feliciano went with a few unfortunate workmen to a ravine near the castle. He was showing them where to do some work. Right then he saw some armed men, but the Baron didn't think they were bandits. You know, around there we've never had any trouble like this before. They came up to him and asked him if he was the Baron Spandolieri.

"'I am,' the poor man answered. Immediately they surrounded them. 'We only want money,' they told the Baron. Then they took the two of them to the castle and sent the young Baronello in with a letter. They demanded fifty thousand lira from the Baroness. Imagine! Fifty thousand! They waited outside the door, but when it opened the Baronello came out shooting at them. He didn't hit any of the bandits, but they got him at the temple, singed his head. Next they shot at the people in the windows. When the Baroness saw this business, she gave them the money. She sent her chaplain to give them the fifty thousand lira. They took the ransom, freed the Baron Spandolieri, and left. But now listen to this: in an hour's time they came back to the castle and ransacked all the apartments, breaking the furniture and everything they saw. They left with two hundred fifty thousand lira and whatever objects they liked. One of the thieves came back with a gold watch, saying he didn't want trinkets.

"No doubt they are the *maledetti* who killed Pasquale. The *carabinieri* have received the inside word. They know who the Boss is. Just last week they killed two of the gang; it was a five-hour battle in the mountains. The others escaped. There are at least seven left. Since Pasquale, no one has heard a word of them. Where can they be hiding? No one knows. The word is that these are the same murderers who kidnapped the good Dr. Serafini."

This Cousin interested me. I saw at once that he had "serious intentions." Of course, he did not say anything about them or put out empty boasts. He was a giant of a man, well over six-three. His boys were tall, too, but not as tall as their father. They were quiet as he told the story, while the others agreed, showed shock, cursed all by way of helping the cousin tell his story. I said nothing. By the way he talked, I knew he was waiting for the right sign, the right moment to act. He himself was known as a sharpshooter. It was said he could hit a moving target accurately at twenty-three meters. After he told his story, no one asked him anything. In our town everyone knows everything already anyway. It's a great comfort, not having to say the obvious.

There was one part of the story he didn't tell, since everybody knew it. It was about Dr. Serafini, a saintly medical doctor, who for years helped everyone in his village. If you couldn't pay, there was no question he would still treat you. One day last spring the bandits had a shootout with the *carabinieri* in which their Boss was wounded. That night they kidnapped Dr. Serafini from his bed, telling his wife she should not worry, they would bring him right back. They kept him five months; and after he cured the Boss they brought this saint to the outskirts of his town and killed him there on the crossroads. After his funeral his wife, children, and whole family moved to the Continent.

On the way out of the wake, I turned back to look at the Cousin and our eyes met for a long second. When the door closed behind me I felt lonely, but better. Where was I going to sleep? Not home, not now. My brothers had probably told my parents that I was working for an old man who lived out of town, as I sometimes did. And since I usually slept there they hadn't started to look for me yet, but my mother would soon smell a rat. I went to the blacksmith's barn and I made a bed for myself in the hayloft beside a window where I could see the front door across the yard. I was really hungry and ate another small prickly pear. Soon it was dark. Once the door opened and I saw the light coming from inside the house and the blacksmith came out to grill the family's dinner. He did all the familiar things that I had seen people do since I could remember, but as I watched him carefully I felt as though I were watching a priest at an altar, maybe I mean an actor on a stage. The blacksmith was careful, exact in his motions, and when his work was done he picked up the platter and went inside, leaving only the pile of glowing coals. Just as he crossed the threshold I imagined he would turn and wave.

After a while I fell asleep. I even remember the dream I had: I was on the shore of the great sea and I saw my family living on a raft that was floating away, some mysterious underwave was carrying them from me. I watched them from the shore, but they didn't seem to see me. They were just walking about doing ordinary things as they did at home. I didn't say anything as I watched them slip farther and farther away, but I felt terribly sad. Because of the dream I took the chance of sneaking around my house to just get a glimpse of my mother, but she wasn't there. Even the stove was cold.

I dragged my feet to the Town Hall, knowing the Mayor would be sending me back to the "craftsmen" sooner than I was ready to go. This time he gave me a pouch with two folded pieces of paper in it closed with his usual complication of "official" seals. I got out of town again without meeting anyone, but everyone knew I had been back. (There are more eyes in my town than tongues.) I found the right turn in the road to the farmhouse.

One of the men met me, saying he had been watching me walk on the road below for a full twenty minutes before he recognized me. "It's a good thing I saw it was you, Kid," he said, following me into the farmhouse. From his expression I could see that the Boss was "thinking" about me. I had to really watch out now that my messenger business was nearly over. I was becoming an annoying fly who had unfortunately found its way to his face.

"Boss," I said after I delivered the pouch, "I left my house for good today and would like to join you here."

"You plan to join us? That's nice. What do we want with you?"

"I can be useful."

"Useful? That's funny. What can you do?"

"I can do everything."

"What do you mean, you can do everything?"

"You know, everything. I can do carpentry, painting, I can fix anything." They all laughed at this.

"We're not building houses this month, maybe next." They all laughed and I did, too.

"But I mean I can do everything," I said again, emphasizing "everything."

At that moment the Crazy One looked at me with a

bad smirk and suddenly smacked me so hard that I tumbled backward, and then to my surprise he smiled and walked away. Instead of standing up, I ran for his legs and threw him over. It wasn't what you would call thought out. I took my chance. He had a pistol at my head.

"Too much, too much," shouted the woman, moving in front of me and pulling me up by my shirt. I felt like a kitten being moved. "Gino, this kid can be useful to me. Get that crazy bastard out of here now," she said.

*Get out*, the Boss gestured to the men, who immediately melted away, including the Crazy One who had slapped me. The three of us were left—no, the two of them were left and I was dangling between them.

"What do you want with this idiot?" asked the Boss.

"I can use him in the farmhouse, especially, considering . . ." she said, looking the Boss in the face.

He turned away, making a gesture to her that lightened my heart. It meant, *leave me out of this; it's your business*. With that he started to walk out the door.

When the Boss was almost out, he suddenly turned to me. "If you were joining us, where's your stuff?"

"What stuff? Do I look as though I have stuff? I don't own anything."

"You've got weasel smarts and you're a fast talker, Kid, but I don't like talkers. Are your eyes and ears as good as your tongue?"

I turned my eyes away and remained perfectly still for a long time. The room was very, very quiet. I heard a loud *poo-poo-poo*, a handsome Hoopoe was calling nearby. Then again, *up-up-upidae*. The Boss turned and walked out the door. That's how I came to live with them.

# 3: LIVING IN THE PLACE

☙

As soon as we were alone, the Missus, as I called her, said to me, "My name is Immaculata, so don't call me, Missus, Auntie, or Grandmother." And without thinking I said, "And I'm called by a number of names: Little Thirteen, Joseph, or Lucky." She picked "Kid," and that was that. "Listen, Kid, that small one who slapped you, he's completely crazy. U Pazzu is what everyone calls him. If you see him coming—run. Do you understand? Run. Don't think you can trick him or fight him. Next to Gino, he's the worst. With Gino you might have a minute to talk, but the crazy one is a human who doesn't reason, can't reason, has no respect for anything. He has nothing to guide him. Nothing natural is behind him, so nothing good is in front of him. And he hates children."

"That reminds me of a man in my town who was never allowed out of the house without at least two of his brothers with him. What sort of humans are these anyway? Thanks for the advice."

"I don't give 'advice,'" she answered. "I'm more of a sign painter, if you see what I mean." She looked at me closely, hesitated for a second, shook her head, grunted loudly, and walked away, the old pistol in the folds of her skirt. "Don't try to figure him out. He's dangerous, that's all you need to know."

Why was she there with them? Maybe she was someone's sister or mother, but I never found out; maybe she was related to someone who had been killed or maybe she was a stand-in for someone else, someone she was protecting. Of course, I never asked, and I never found out. I saw that she knew things. She liked all little and new creatures. I once saw her save a nest of mice. She dealt easily with the constant and surprising inconveniences that young people and life bring. More than once she said that as a "snot-nose" (*muccarusu chi si*) I was especially inconvenient. She noticed everything. Once, not meaning to, I mimicked her Palermo accent and she heard it right away, stopped, turned, and, narrowing her eyes, looked at me. "Quit that, kid. It's not necessary."

The ruin was just one big room with a small lean-to that had a big cooking stove and a sink. We had a good cistern, which I expected would cave the roof in, but while I was there it never did. All kinds of herbs were drying in bundles on the walls of the lean-to. She had made a corner room for herself by putting up a curtain, and that night she found a rag of a curtain for me. We put it up in a corner so that now I, too, had a room. She also found a mattress, and I fixed that falling-apart chair, and that was that. Although the mattress sported some mountains and valleys, it had no insect life in it, which was more than I could say for myself.

"Having head lice is nothing, just ordinary," she barked. "We can remedy the situation."

"Thank you, very much," I said, bowing my lethal head of hair.

"What are you doing? Don't feel ashamed. Never mind, never mind. Having lice is not a shame. It's nothing. It's only natural."

With all her barking, you might have thought she was mad at you, but actually she was baring her teeth at the lice, like a dog nipping, in systematic rows, at the lousy parts of his own skin. In those days most people still lived as though we were all one skin. She wasn't scandalized by real lice or by my shaved head, which cured me and made me look like a proper convict. I hoped it wasn't an omen of things to come.

There was a niche on one of the walls with nothing in

it, but beside it was a picture of Saint Agatha, and she had a lit candle in front of it; Sant' Agatuzza was definitely our patron saint. That night, lying in bed, I watched the candlelight flickering on the ceiling and the room wasn't rubble, or a hopeless ruin. Soon after, as I was lying there half dreaming, I heard the door open.

"What do you want?" said a strained voice.

"Wait, I'll come outside."

(I have excellent hearing so I heard them as clearly as if they were still in the room.)

"Gino, keep that one away from here."

"What can I do? I'll tell him to stay away, but you know he's crazy."

"He's sick. I don't want him around the boy."

"That kid's pushing his luck."

"He's only a kid and he's a good worker. Besides, he could be your son."

"Yeah, but he isn't, is he? And you know it. ["Thee knows it," he said. With her he always used the respectful term *Vossia*.] I don't know if I can afford to let him go.

"Each time a plague comes down on you."

"A plague? To hell with plagues. I, I am the plague. Let the bastards understand that now I am the plague. You can have this kid around for now, but don't get too used to him, because if I smell he's still connected, I'm going to get rid of him, and that will be that. Do you understand?"

"I've seen something that is . . ." Her voice trailed away, and I heard their steps and her voice fade until I couldn't make out what they were saying. In that quiet and mysterious night, I lay there thinking, I am connected, but for the life of me, I couldn't remember to what.

I lived with them for a little more than nine months in a world that was the cut-out side of our ordinary one, different yet strangely familiar. For example, the gang spoke only about goods and money, goods and money, so you'd think they were proper businessmen instead of robbers and murderers. Sometimes they sounded like smug merchants. I shuddered when I overheard them talking about people, situations, and dates that only someone in the family or village could know. How did they know so much? Was it only the Mayor who had dealings with them? They exchanged their real life for money and goods until all that surrounded them was a collection of dead things, and it was in, with, and about these dead things that they moved in spurts of violence.

Many outlaws, 'Mmaculata told me, started with a single act of desperation, usually having to do with food and need, or some violence committed in their family, but once they were outside the law, that was that. You're in, you're out. With this group, "out" had happened a long time ago. Their old anger grew like bad plants in a good pond until finally all the water was choked. Since they were always either angry or very angry, you could not really know from one minute to the next what they would do. They lived by no peaceful order or habit; neither the heat of the sun nor what my mother would have called, "reasons of the heart" moved them; so, having fallen away from nature and society, they were surrounded by chaos, which 'Mmaculata called hell. Whenever they were around, I knew my life wasn't worth much; and whenever I was alone, I knew my freedom wasn't worth much. If the police captured them I would probably be going to prison. My brothers had really sent me to the Ogres' house.

Even as a boy I had no illusions. Here at least I was managing to eat delicious *minestra*, and I had good work each day and a bed. Back home my family, I imagined, was still hungry. God knows what my oldest brothers had told my parents, not that it would be easy to fool them, especially my mother. Words didn't convince her. She had other means of knowing. Whatever ways of saving me that my father would think of would have to do with intelligence and endurance, not violent action. At first I expected them to come and save me. But after a while I did not think or worry about my old life. Keeping alive was hard enough and I needed to keep all my strength, which worry saps. I had learned that early. For the time being, my real life was now inside out.

In my family's rhythm of life I had followed the natural daily routine that everyone in town followed, which all the beings in the world follow. You always knew when people were eating or working or sleeping or waking. Each day brought the sun and our work, and night brought the moon and stars and our sleep. But now I purposely changed my life, so that even ordinary things were turned upside down. Sometimes, instead of sleeping in bed, I'd stretch out under it or on the bench or in a corner or outside. That way I got to see things differently. Once I was actually saved from the Crazy One by simply not being where he had expected, and at another time I was so mixed into a pile of pots that while he kept searching my blankets I sat frozen, with my head down, and he luckily never saw me.

At first I could feel the moments before the terrible split-second silence of danger, and then I began to anticipate their erratic coming and the violence it always brought, so that I could leave beforehand or get out of its way in a split second. I learned to hide inside silences, to disappear without a word or a footprint. Like a jack-in-the-box, I jumped down inside the place. It was in the dark that I began to see. But it was cooking with 'Mmaculata, walking into new fields, and climbing in the mountains above the ruin that made me content with my life, and strange as it is to write this: it is true that when I was not in immediate danger, I was truly happy.

Most of the time I did not know where the gang was and what they were doing. There was the Boss, the Crazy One, the Basil Man, three brothers from Girgenti, who diminished in size as well as in age and name—Small, Smaller, Smallest—and the look-out man. A few times I was asked to replace the lookout, whose name was Santo, but they called him Generale Caduti Massi, which of course was ironic. It was said there was no one like him: when he was sitting on the mountain he could see a rabbit twitch its whiskers down in the valley, but if he got up and walked, he stumbled, fell, usually breaking something. He simply couldn't walk without smashing into something, and it didn't matter if he was inside a house or out on a mountain road. When I replaced him that first time, he told me, "Your job is to watch this path as far as you can see. Once in a while, look around the Cat Boulders." This last instruction he called back to me over his shoulder. "Watch them! Watch them!" All the while cursing softly to himself as he went back and forth on the narrow path, all the while slipping, displacing great stones, which tumbled down the mountain, until finally he himself disappeared around the Boulders at the third turn.

"I forgot to leave you the gun," his bodiless voice came up to me. "It doesn't work anyway. If you see someone, hide or run back for help."

Clouds of dust and great rocks fell after him. Now, I

understood why they called him Generale Caduti Massi. The signs, ATTENZIONE! CADUTI MASSI, alerting travelers to the possibility of fallen boulders, were still in place, except for the one that had been crushed by one of his landslides. But the funny thing was that when Caduti wasn't moving he was skilled at sitting perfectly still for hours and hours and hours and spotting anything that moved.

"I like to sit and not think or whistle or spit or anything," he once told me. "Moving disturbs my peace."

He hardly ever came with the others to eat at the farmhouse, so I always imagined him up there sitting on his mountain. Once, when I brought him something 'Mmaculata had made for him to eat, I saw that he was sitting with his eyes half closed.

"Hey, Santo, wake up. 'Mmaculata sent you something special today, wake up."

"Wake up? What do you mean, boy? I am awake. When I am looking slant and relaxed I see everything better. Remember that, Joseph. When you are not looking for something directly, more things present themselves to your sight. Try it yourself and see."

When I got back to the ruin, I asked 'Mmaculata, "How did the General get here? Does he go out with the others? What's the story?"

"Aaah," she answered, "who knows too much is obliged to talk."

"Seriously, tell me about Santo."

She looked at me for a minute and then shook her head sadly. "Gino found him on a mountain path when he was a baby, wrapped in an old jacket, all covered with stone dust. He was about a year old, an unfortunate, probably left by someone who couldn't feed him anymore. He must have been there for a while, not moving, not crying. He was leaning against a boulder, sitting where he had been left, his eyes wide open, quiet as a stone. He's been here with them ever since that day. Gino just picked him up."

Nothing came or went from there that the gang didn't know about. How did they come across the mountain farm? Was Gino a son come home? How did they know so much about our town? The bandits did not live with us at the farmhouse; I now began looking for their hideout. At first I just went out for an hour each day, and then I went out for longer, and then a little longer. The fields and the mountains became my real home. Whenever I wasn't fixing things or cooking, I was out walking. Even at siesta, which we call *l'otta di lu chaudu*, the time of heat, I didn't go back to the house but slept against trees, once in a while my familiar chestnut tree. The neutral trees, beautiful and indifferent to my fate, gave me another life. It was with them that I lived in the great world without humans and their miserable problems. I felt reverent in the presence of that old chestnut.

Don't get me wrong, I also loved being at the farmhouse, which held my past and future. It was there I helped 'Mmaculata prepare meals, which were always at erratic times.

"You're a crazy army," she would say to Gino when they showed up. And he always answered, "So you're ready to leave on a forced march with us?"

"I'm not going anywhere just yet."

Then she would look at what they brought us to cook, and she'd tell me what was needed to start our cooking. They were a hungry group, and never in my whole life, not before or after, have I ever eaten as much as I did in those months. 'Mmaculata loved to cook, and by helping her I learned something new every day. We had our own bread oven, which I had not recognized when I first saw the stone heap. We baked bread a few times a week and grilled all kinds of roasted meats on the usual charcoal stove outside the lean-to. Each meal was a surprise. I ate things I had never eaten before: cheeses that were tastier than anything imaginable, like *ricotta salata* with oranges and walnuts, and I got to be able to judge good provolone, which we ate with onion bread and little tasty black olives. Since before this I had hardly eaten any meat, all the meat roasts were firsts for me, but 'Mmaculata and I thought the men's taste for meat was exaggerated. They ate it all the time. We even ate fish regularly, and it was not a penny's barter of tuna under oil or the ubiquitous dry cod. But even the dry cod 'Mmaculata prepared in many delicious ways. I had never liked *baccalà* before this. She could make a dish out of anything that was around.

"Where do they get fresh fish up here?" I asked one evening.

"Stop asking so many questions, just look and learn. And if or when you are out of here, do the opposite in some things and the same in others."

"Which is which?"

"Stop kidding, you don't have that luxury."

"I think it's the only one I do have." At this she laughed and slapped me on the back.

I went back to starting the fire for roasting. You'd think I would have been so worried I couldn't eat, but that wasn't the case. Maybe I was too young to be a worrier, but I've seen babies who were worried before they could say Mama or Papa. I guess worrying wasn't in my nature. Whatever the reason, I enjoyed every meal 'Mmaculata made, from beginning to end. Once, when the provisions were low, she caught a rabbit, which she marinated in vinegar for longer than I wanted to wait. I even asked her to make a pot of those chickpeas again.

"Don't get sentimental on me. You can't afford it," she

said. "There you'd be feeling all good about those dear, old chickpeas and not paying attention, and someone might have just sneaked in here and "adjusted" the taste so that you'd never eat chickpeas again, and then where would you be? As it is, your future is being cooked in a leaky pot."

"I can fix leaky pots," I answered cockily. She gave me that oh-you-pathetic-kid shake of the head.

"I hope so," she growled, "I really hope so."

But with all that joking I still kept out of the Crazy One's way. I shuddered every time I saw or felt him looking at me. She was right, he was worse than the boss. Once he bit his knuckle and threw me the vindictive kiss, that silent threat that says, *I haven't forgotten you and someday I'm going to get you!*

Whenever the gang crossed the threshold I could hear a terrible hum. It was a really deafening hum. "Don't bother figuring it out," 'Mmaculata said when she saw that I heard it. "Listen and you'll hear sounds like that everywhere. Everything, everything. This world is full of sounds, everything is humming or making some kind of music, the big stars and the planets, the sun and the moon, even trees are sometimes in harmony, which you can hear. Each tree has its own sound with and without the wind and if you listen carefully, even the stones speak."

I had been there for months when one beautiful morning 'Mmaculata woke me by bringing me *caffe latte cu li fidduzzi*, the usual big cup of coffee and hot milk with broken pieces of nice hard bread in it.

"Get up!" she whispered loudly in that raspy voice. "Get up! Do you know what a wild asparagus looks like? This is the right time for them on the mountainside. I can feel them out there. Today, you're going to find them in the fields."

"Asparagus?" I said. "I am an expert on finding asparagus. There are patches around my house that know my name."

"Cut it out, kid," she said, laughing. "I don't have time to waste on this kind of stuff this morning. Have some coffee. We're making *lasagneddi cu li sparaciddi.*"

I spent hours searching for wild asparagus up in the mountain meadows, climbing higher and higher. The beautiful Sicilian spring day made me feel drunk. In the middle of the highest field I picked a few stalks, and just as I was adding the last to my collection I heard the scattered tinkling of sheep bells. And then from someplace I heard a whistling sound—a shepherd's pipe. I followed the music until I saw the shepherd playing his pipe, sitting on an outcropping below, his back to me. I walked out of sight and lay on the blessed ground, and for the longest time I listened to the music. I can't tell you how long I stayed there, for time was lost; and when suddenly the music stopped, I heard a great rush of *tlee tlee tling*ing of tiny sheep bells and I finally stood up to see, below, the shepherd and his flock—a vast crowd now moving quickly down the mountain.

By the time I came home I had two beautiful bunches of wild asparagus, which I had tied with thread into bouquets like flowers, thin, thin, and very dark green. Their wild fragrance like nothing planted in rows. As I handed them to 'Mmaculata she said, "They deserve the best garlic and cheese, but first we have to make the dough for the *lasagneddi*, the thin flat pasta that goes with the oil, garlic, and asparagus. To begin, you must make the dough from good flour and good water, but the real secret is in your hands and how you handle the knife while cutting the dough. If it is right you will always hear the same music: *tsikita, tsikita, tsikita.*"

*Tsikita, tsikita, tsikita*, went the kitchen knife, cutting the folded dough into perfect flat noodles. *Tsikita, tsikita, tsikita*, went the morning, and in the end we had a long string of not-too-thin *lasagneddi* drying. Later we made a whole pot of them and ate them with the wild asparagus, oil, and garlic. Beautiful thin asparagus growing on the mountainside in the middle of all that human evil. They were some of the first green things I saw there, so you see it was in March, when everything has hope but is holding danger as well. My father used to say each year, "March sits like a knife, bitter winter on one side and spring on the other." *Tsikita, tsikita, tsikita* went my life.

One day when we were working together in a field, she stopped and said, "Keep your eyes open. Keep your young eyes open.": *Tini l'occhi aperti.*

"What," I said, "are we looking for? More asparagus?"

"Don't make stupid jokes about this," she said. "Unless you're cooler than a snake, or your luck is really as good as it looks, you'd better keep your eyes open."

"So I can watch where I step?" I said, seeing the little viper she was talking about move so fast I couldn't tell what rock it slithered under.

Then, for a fillip, she added, "It's keeping your eyes open that makes the good luck want to stay around you."

After a while I said, "Well, I can't even figure where the horses are kept." I had only just discovered a path down to a meadow and an old outbuilding that could be gotten to from a back road, a place that could have been used for the animals.

"*Cu vidi chiu di lu padrunu e urvu,*" she answered. Who sees more than the owner is blind.

"Ah! It's true. You do know my mother."

"Just keep alert so that you know before they decide you are not doing things in their interest," she said seriously. "Watch for any sudden shift in the air, sometimes it's as small as dust moving, with no sound at all. Learn to see that or you won't get the chance to hear your mother teach you more of the old sayings. And another thing: it's better that they don't show you where they live because once they do, you're either in or out."

"Oh! Just like my brothers."

"What do you mean?"

"Nothing," I answered. "That's an old story."

"I hope this is not a case of 'I speak and my boots listen,'" she added, just to get a new one in.

"No, I am paying attention, 'Mmaculata."

("I speak and my boots listen," was a saying my wise and loving Godfather FoFò used to say to us boys.)

'Mmaculata taught me to cook, to love the fruits of the earth, and even one glorious day how to ride a horse. I was learning other things from the highwaymen.

After for a while when 'Mmaculata and I had not seen them, the gang began to show up at the farmhouse to eat every day. On the first night while I was in bed, I heard 'Mmaculata talking to one of the men. Was it Santo? He was agitated, she was calm. They talked for a long time and I fell asleep to their droning voices. Then one afternoon I unexpectedly turned up at the farmhouse and saw through the kitchen window Immaculata talking at the table with Santo, and he was crying. She was comforting him; she was something else, all right. Then he kissed her hand and she blessed him and he left. When I saw her an hour later, she seemed unusually cheerful.

"Where's he going?" I even surprised myself with that question. As usual, she didn't answer when I asked questions about the gang, but after that I understood from their talk at dinner that no one had seen him for a few days, which was not unusual.

"Maybe one of those Boulders finally buried him," said the oldest of the three Girgenti brothers. (All three of the brothers were dark, with those blue-gray Sicilian eyes.)

"Poor Santo," said another of the brothers.

"We should have a mass said for him," said the third. Everyone laughed.

The gang didn't show up for a whole week and then two, and when they didn't come back after the third week, I began to hope that they were permanently gone. But they were there again late one afternoon and with a great appetite. In no time 'Mmaculata came out with a huge pot and carefully ladled the food out onto the large wooden board that was our old table. The board was chipped at my place and my fork was missing two teeth. That day for the first dish she made macaroni and tomato sauce, and with it a huge mountain of fried eggplant was passed around. Everyone took a slice or two off the top and then cut it into his pasta, topping it with a good sprinkling of hard sheep's cheese.

"Where's the basil?" the man with the broken nose asked. "My father, God rest his soul, always put basil on this."

"It's in front of your nose, can't you smell it?" Gino said, and everyone laughed. I picked up the plate and passed it to him, and when it finally came back to me, there was only one tiny leaf left. I made a mental note to next time put a few leaves on my plate before passing it. Later, I mentioned this to Immaculata.

"So you've finally learned something at that table."

That afternoon, I took water to our patch of basil and as a reward I could smell its strong fragrance.

"Fresh basil is strong, like eggplant," she said. "Sometimes strong and strong go good together, like husbands and wives," she said with a laugh. Once I asked her what she thought about delicate with delicate. She said she didn't know about that, but in her old age she'd like to try that combination.

When the men were at the farmhouse eating, she never sat down with them. Once, when the Basil Man stood up and bowed and asked her to sit down, she shook her head. "Too busy," she said, and walked away. You could tell she liked to eat alone, keep her own counsel, and talk to them only about provisions. If you had lived there, you would have known never to ask her anything about anything. She gave stony looks as answers, even if you hadn't asked the question that was on your mind. It was a great place to figure things out for yourself. Although until then I had been saved through her good graces, I knew they would "attempt the deed" (as 'Mmaculata called it) when she was not around. They would make sure of that. It was just as she said, "You cannot guess the moment." Even now I can hear her saying, "What do you want to be certain about? Only the 'always uncertain' need to know for sure."

ONE COLD AFTERNOON, while I was walking in a meadow, I heard the shepherd's pipe again, and I lay down in the yellow grass to listen as though I had not one care in the world. It was a haunting song with sounds like mountain winds. Then came dances fit for a wedding. And soon something unexpected, more intense than the first tunes, swept me up. When the music ended, I felt my raggedy life filled with a beauty I had not recognized before. I moved down the mountainside carefully to avoid stepping on the tiny colonies of delicate moss and spring flowers growing in those stony fields.

As I said, it was only the grace of God shown through 'Mmaculata's interest in me that kept me safe for the moment, and it was to that moment that I was completely faithful. As a child I had lived inside my own life with whatever I had found there, so I never imagined life as separate from my family, but now I saw and heard something new, something greater than my small life, something that had been created. And for a moment I felt like a lone seer, a discoverer. But when I came back to myself I saw what I had discovered brought me simply to a greater home which at the moment included murderers and robbers and a saving angel. I could not refute it. The world with its thousands of beautiful things had come to me there, in that place, at that time, even with the pain and danger around me. My young heart felt it and knew it. The shepherd's music had shown me both the sickness and the remedy.

In our village a person is quite grown up at thirteen, which for me was March 19, St. Joseph's Day, about the time I went looking for the wild asparagus and first heard the shepherd's music. This mountain and fields meant so much to me that I returned whenever I could. One afternoon a month later I was lucky to see the flock and hear the shepherd's pipe again. He played a long time and when the music stopped, the bellwether ran past me and soon the *tling tling tling* of the flock and, sure enough right on their heels, the shepherd in his cloak surprised me.

"Hello," I called loudly before he saw me. I stood still and watched him as he turned.

"Hello. I was wondering what was in their path." And to my surprise I saw not a man but a young boy looking at me.

"My name is Joseph," I said, "and I live down there." I pointed to the valley below and then extended my hand.

"Hello. My name is Bettina."

"Bettina?" I asked stupidly, cupping my ear quickly with the insolent hand, pretending I had not heard her, giving myself time to recover. I was so surprised and embarrassed that I felt myself blushing. She had luminous gray eyes, very black thick eyelashes, and lovely dark eyebrows. On her right temple she had a small, deep scar.

"Yes, Bettina. You know, Elizabetta," she said with dignity, then pointed to a green field above us. "I can't tarry. I have to hurry after them." I tried keeping up for a while, but when I couldn't see them anymore, I gave up and went back home.

After meeting her, I doubled my walks on the mountain and was rewarded; I learned that for each spring and summer her sheep grazed until fall in these mountain fields. During all the times we met, we only said a few things to each other, yet we felt comfortable in each other's company. She was fourteen and lived with her grandparents and two brothers. When she was six her parents had died of a fever within weeks of each other. She had a lively quiet about her and when the sheep were grazing we sat together. Once she told me that I had very good manners. She said her brothers had been to a great city at Christmas to play flute and bagpipes and they had seen many different kinds of exciting people. She herself was extremely courteous in her sparse speech and predictable ways, sharing her meal, which was always cheese and bread wrapped carefully in a napkin carried in the deep inside pocket of her large cloak. She did everything in the same measured and sure way, even the cutting of the cheese and bread. A few times I brought something modest from the farmhouse, but she always shook her head and said, "No, thank you." We carried water from a spring to our little flat stone table, and once I offered some greens that I had gathered, which she was glad to take home. When we finished eating (we met many times, but this time not one word had been spoken), she stretched out on the grass and I saw her thin dark arms stretch out from her cape and I lay down next to her, stretched out on the earth like her, and for a second our fingertips touched. She did not move and we stayed that way for an eternity, and then something shifted and a patch of cold bright moss was between our fingers. She sat up quickly, put her hands over her gray eyes, and I watched her stand, shake herself as though she had grown feathers, then like a beautiful eagle turn her head way around to look keenly at something in the distance, and in seconds on some mysterious and silent signal, she and the flock flew away.

# 4: FINDING THE STABLES

ఠ

OUR DAYS at the farmhouse were quiet—"Too quiet," warned 'Mmaculata. Then one morning the Basil Man came to get us. "Follow me. The Boss is sending you to get provisions." We followed and after being around them for six months, I finally saw where they lived. It was a series of falling-down stables, north and below the farmhouse, set way back in a desolate place, so hidden that I don't think I would have found it easily on my own. "Be careful, Carù," she said when we were alone. "There's a reason for this. Have you figured it out?"

While 'Mmaculata and the others were talking, I walked through the back door of the small, stinking stable to a pen filled with abandoned stuff. My eyes went naturally to a cart; it was Pasquale's, and then, to break my heart again, I saw a donkey standing alone in the corner. It was Artù. The poor thing was skin and bones. "Artù," I called, and he looked up; "Artù," and he walked toward me. His eyelids were covered with huge flies. I put my arms around his neck and he nestled his nose in the crook of my arm.

Pasquale had always been respectful to animals. Even now I can hear him say, "Hold on, Joseph, I'm coming, but the animals must eat first." The stable was a filthy place, filled with manure, bad air, and the miserable debris of stealing. I looked around and among the broken and thrown-out objects, once precious to others, I found a bag of grain and was giving the donkey some when 'Mmaculata called me.

"Later, Artù, I'll come back and take care of you later," I crooned to him while he was eating. I gave him another handful, closed the bag, and put it back where I had found it. He looked up at me. I felt bad leaving him like that. "Later, Artù," I promised again. "Later," I said, already walking out the door, but I knew that "later" is not a word for creatures or saints.

Immaculata and I picked up a horse and cart and were told to drive to a general store in Canicattì, which I remembered as Pasquale's cousin's town. Just before we left, the Boss gave 'Mmaculata a bag and a piece of paper.

I knew what was in the bag, which she put inside her skirt pocket, but I wasn't sure about the paper.

"What's on the list in your pocket?"

"List? What do I need a list for? Here's where I keep lists," she said, tapping her forehead.

"And your pocket is where you keep the money."

"Metal, base metal, that's what's in this pocket, Kid."

"I know. I know. 'Coins are nothing but base metal,' my father used to say. 'They are are nothing more than dead stuff. But, of course, you can't really say that 'living gold and silver' is stuff, since it is not in the world of stuff, not even in a world where stuff exists." (I was on a roll.)

"I understand, I understand," she said, laughing.

"Did I ever tell you my father was a poet? We understood that the mind and heart are the 'living silver' and the 'living gold,'" I said, wildly flinging my hand to my head and chest and then back again. (In those days I could really get into things.)

"Careful, Kid, if you don't pay close attention to that curve up ahead, all this jabbering and head-scratching won't matter."

She was right. The road was treacherous, so I settled down into just driving, something Pasquale had taught me to do well.

"Those poets are good word sneaks," she said later.

"What?"

"I'm sorry I never met your father the poet. You're a good driver, Kid."

"My friend Pasquale taught me," I said, settling down.

We drove the next hour in silence, entering the town as the municipal clock was striking twelve. At that hour in any town people move around a lot before going home to sit down at table. In the square three old men were talking excitedly, waving their arms, shaking their heads, agreeing or disagreeing, I couldn't tell which. One minute they were all silent, and then some spark and again they were on fire. I wondered what they were so passionate about. At the far end, a young woman was balancing two big round loaves of bread, and above her a tiny woman on a balcony was calling her children home, and in the next building, at a closed window, an ancient woman in a pure white dress and cap was sitting, no, not quite sitting, maybe fallen to the side, like a porcelain doll placed against a satin pillow. Right below her, at the side exit of a school, I saw a line of boys being dismissed. They were in a perfect line until they got out the door. I remembered my brothers and me. Maybe a hundred years had passed since those days.

"Turn here," 'Mmaculata told me. We left the square and drove on a wide side street that brought us in front of the store. There was no mistaking it. "Stop gawking," she said. I tied the horse and cart and gave the feed bag and two coins to a boy, who agreed to bring water and look after things. When I put the coins into his small hand, I knew it could once have been mine.

'Mmaculata was already climbing the stairs when I caught up with her, and together we entered the immense store. We exchanged greetings with four customers standing at the counter. When my eyes got accustomed to the dark, I saw the entire place was lined with shelves that were filled with goods, in sacks, bales, tins, crates, and a few feet away were huge jars, some as tall as a man. It was impressive. The merchant, I heard later, was said to be one of those people who sold so many goods that his fortune had no bottom. *Stu mircanti vinnia robba; comu vinnia robba era un riccuni di chiddi 'n funnu.* I had never been in a place like it, and if I hadn't felt awe in the old temples at Girgenti, I would have felt awe here, for the sight of such accumulation amazed me. There was so much stuff that I felt dizzy at the sight of it.

"Close your mouth, Kid, you're catching flies," 'Mmaculata whispered.

The huge place was dark, and so cool it was almost cold. Where were we? We had entered another world, one that I had never seen before, did not understand, and did not trust. My stomach felt queasy.

While Immaculata and I were standing near the counter awaiting our turn, the bell rang and the front door opened and shut quietly, quietly behind us and someone said, "*Salve.*" It was a voice I had heard before, and there right behind us was Pasquale's cousin saying, "*Salve,*" again, but this time to us. I was surprised and not surprised. Everyone exchanged the time of day; the Cousin bent his head to acknowledge Immaculata. I saw that he had recognized me, but he said nothing to me as he came up to the counter next to me. I said hello and no more. The merchant did not ask Immaculata any personal questions. You know the kind: *Where are you from? How long are you staying? Do you know such and such?* The talk was polite and spare, nothing frivolous or rude. Immaculata told the merchant what we needed, the quantity, and then said the name of the item once, *farina,* which was repeated for comprehension, *farina,* and then by the clerk for its physical presence on the counter or at our feet, *farina.* What a huge pile! We were there past closing time. We got everything we had come for, except for some threads of saffron. "Not until next season," the merchant said. 'Mmaculata and the merchant did not discuss the price of anything, in itself strange; we paid what was asked, whereupon a large discount was given, and we left. Even about the simplest things, I still had a lot to learn.

The Cousin, the merchant's man, the boy, and I loaded the wagon without exchanging a word. Then the man and boy went back inside, and just as I put in the last sack of flour in the back of the cart, the Cousin came close to me, looked up at the sky, and said, "I think it's going to rain."

"Well, that's good," I said. "It's been very dry up at our place. We could use the rain, although it will make a mess; we have piles and piles of donkey manure. It'll be a stinking mess, all right." (I have no idea now, nor did I then, why I said that.)

"*Ah! Merda,*" he said.

"Yeah," I answered.

"And to think it's donkey shit?" he asked.

"Yes, donkey shit, what else would it be?" I answered.

Then the Cousin just walked away. My heart sank. I almost called out, but he was already inside the store. If my salvation was to come from this ordinary world and its inhabitants, I would not have guessed it then. My own world was not theirs.

When I got into the cart 'Mmaculata said, "Someone from the gang is certainly watching us. You talked to that big man twice as long as you needed to. When giving directions, learn to be brief." I didn't answer. What could I say? I looked around, but the streets were now empty, except for those three old men still in the same place, still talking passionately. Weren't they ever going home? As we turned the corner and came close to them, I still couldn't make out the drift of their words.

"Immaculata, what are those men talking about?"

"Fava beans," she said.

"Fava beans? Not really."

"Really."

"And when we came into town, what were they talking about?"

"Fava beans."

"Are you sure?"

"I'm sure."

"What's so special about fava beans?"

"For one thing, they're good food, and the old stories say that the fava plant holds the place between this earth and the underworld."

"Ah! Yeah, now I see. Fava beans definitely hold a place between this world right here and the other one you go to when you don't have any fava beans to eat."

"Don't joke about food, Kid. Many families live on fava beans. My mother once said that her grandmother had twelve ways of preparing them, and that was only the beginning. Tomorrow you can get us bunches of wild fennel that are out in the south field—and I'll teach you a new dish instead of those chickpeas you like so much."

"Thanks," I said.

On the ride back I thought over my situation, which had turned from bad to terminal. The Boss had purposely shown me where they really lived. Now I knew too much, just like the good Dr. Serafini. 'Mmaculata had said that I was either "in or out." I needed temporary measures. Be useful. Maybe I could patrol with Santo at the Boulders?

Perhaps it had already been decided; only the time and place remained a question. Perhaps my leaky pot was beyond repair. I smiled at the thought.

"The real trouble is that I know where they live, so, what the hell!" I said to 'Mmaculata.

"At least you've got the geography right," she said.

When we got to our farmhouse, the three brothers from Girgenti were waiting for us. After everything was unloaded, I brought the horse and cart all the way back to the stables along the easy road. The men did not follow me and I was surprised to find no one at the hideout. I took care of the horse and went to find Artù. After I gave him water, brushed him, and fed him, I put him into a small fenced meadow where a single gray horse was grazing. He and the horse were glad to see each other. Donkeys hate to be alone. I cleaned up the stable a little and looked around.

Across the field, there was a small house and a barn with a large cistern on its roof. I casually walked over and called out, but no one answered. I waited, called again, and then stepped inside the house. The first room had nine bedrolls and a foul smell. Off their room was a small hall at the end of which was a closed door, which I opened and walked into a bedroom, no doubt Gino's, which had a bed and a beautiful chestnut bureau. On the *cantaranu* was a photograph of a woman and two small boys, taken by a photographer in Caltanissetta. Beside it was a candle that had never been lit. Behind a locked door was probably the room filled with their stolen booty. At the far end of the house was another empty stable filled with flies buzzing in and out of a beam of hot afternoon sun. As I slipped out a half-opened door, I saw Small, the oldest of the Girgenti brothers, come up out of the orchard. He was preoccupied and hadn't yet seen me.

"Small, hello. Hello, Small," I called out.

"What are you doing here?"

"I just came back with the horse and cart. Gino told 'Mmaculata and me to get provisions in town."

"Yeah, I know, I know." He looked at me hard and wanted to say something else, but thought better of it. I hate that moment: someone is about to say something and everything is working together, you know, the mind, heart, and tongue—not a space between them—and then you see that change in the eyes. The three scatter, the eyes go blank, the tongue stops, and more likely than not you're done for.

"What?" I asked. "What is it, Small?"

He hesitated then said, "Get outta here, kid. Just get outta here."

The next time I went to the stables I finally found my "boundary." It was a stand of four large cactuses where I could hide and check for signs of the men before going to Artù and the other creatures. Sometimes the horses were there and the men were gone, sometimes the horses were gone and the men were there. If the men were there, I hid and later doubled back to the farmhouse. Although once I was almost caught by the Crazy One, I went secretly to the stables regularly with success. I saw all the places outside the old house: a table under a grape arbor, a makeshift place for a smithy, a garbage pit, and so on. I even knew what grew there. I was beginning to know the land really well now. Once, taking a shortcut up to the farmhouse, I almost slipped off a steep path and was saved by hanging on to a small bush. When I got my footing I saw that I had been saved by a sturdy caper bush whose roots in that dry mountainside went far down, far down. It took me time, but I brought 'Mmaculata a pocket full of capers.

"You worked hard for that pocketful," she said, thanking me. "Go put some olive oil on those hands."

For the better part of the next week no one came up to us at the farmhouse. 'Mmaculata and I were happy and alone again. "Don't dance and sing, Kid. Keep your eyes—" she started, and I finished, "open!" She laughed.

Then one morning just after dawn while I was still in bed, the Boss came and told me to get up and come with him. While I was getting my shirt I heard Immaculata say something to him that I couldn't quite make out. He told her to mind her own business. He told her they had "lost the General."

"I'm going to find the miserable bastard. He picked up and walked away, as if he didn't exist. We can't find a trace of him. Where did he go? He can't just show up in some town; they'll recognize him. Maybe he is discussing the 'meaning of life' with the *sbirri* or, ah!, better still, maybe he went to the *carabinieri* to find his beloved parents who left him to die." He laughed at his own joke. "But wherever he is, the Plague will find the ungrateful bastard."

"Maybe, he's buried down there under the Boulders," she said, walking away.

"Maybe he'd be better off under them than if I catch him. The miserable bastard. So much for your shit about babies and kids."

She shrugged her shoulders. She never gave anyone you-got-me satisfaction. The atmosphere was heavy.

"Who's at the lookout?" I asked cheerfully.

"Why? Do you want to take his place? Hurry up, get dressed, you idiot."

After putting on my shirt, I buckled my new belt and followed him to the door. "Take whatever stuff you need. You'll be staying with us from now on," he said as he opened our rickety door.

"Thanks for the belt, 'Mmaculata."

"Yeah, sure, sure," she said, as she came toward me to give me a kiss, and since she had never done that before, I was alerted. As I kissed her cheek, she whispered, "Your eyes are completely opened," so softly that I couldn't be sure she had even said it. As we walked outside, she handed me a bag with my stuff and followed me out. The bag was heavy, but I knew not to ask her about it in front of the Boss.

When I got a few feet away I turned to wave, but instead I surprised myself and called out, "Bless me, Immaculata." She looked indifferently at me for a long minute as though she were composing herself. Then her entire face changed, and without hesitation she looked right into my eyes with the most compassionate, the most compassionate look I have ever seen in my life. No one had ever looked at me like that before. It was powerful and it lasted a long time, or that's how it felt. When that look of great feeling, of a large caring, went through me, I felt a kind of well-being surrounding me. Before this moment, I had only understood that word "compassion" in terms of deeds and actions. Deeds and actions I under-stood; but a *look* that could change you? Another strange thing was that this intense look did not exactly come from Immaculata. As soon as I felt it, I knew that someone or some thing that was extraordinary had put eyes to a vast source, maybe some great heart, and had looked at me. Whatever it was, I now knew that there could be such a thing. She gave me that blessing before she turned and, without another word, disappeared into the farmhouse. That was the last time I saw Immaculata.

I rode with the Boss down to the stables. The others were waiting with their horses and I doubled with Smallest. "Let's go. We have only an hour." To my surprise, we drove back to the town where Immaculata and I had bought the provisions a few weeks before. Then and there, they held up the merchant with drawn pistols. They told him they wanted all the cash and they had no intention of hurting anyone—unless something went wrong, they said.

Gino told me to go with the merchant to get the cash box. All the while the merchant took me to the hiding place, he said nothing, but when he handed me the box, I saw his hand tremble, and when I almost said some stupid kid thing like *I'm sorry*, he avoided my eyes and looked away and I saw in his eyes a terrible fear for his life. This mirror woke me up. What was I doing with the stupid box in my hands? I looked around for a side door, thinking to grab the poor man and run, but I couldn't see any way out, and when I looked back the Crazy One and Small were watching me from the end of the narrow hall, with their pistols ready and pointing. "Hurry up," Small said. "What the hell are you doing?" For an instant I looked at the merchant. He was staring at me.

I walked back and handed the box to Small. The Crazy One went to the back room—don't ask me why, but I followed him. The merchant was gone—vanished—maybe he was hiding or simply went out a hidden door. Gino called us and we left quickly.

That night I understood what had happened to me. The merchant had carved my face in his memory. I was known as one of them. Now whatever happened to me would be of no consequence to anyone in the honest world, and since I was of no consequence to the gang, I could finally say that I had found a spot where I was invisible. The lovely irony almost got me to laugh. To the honest, half honest, not honest I could completely disappear. Now people would say, "Good riddance to bad rubbish," and make a final sign of the cross between them and me, burying me without pity or regret. You've done a good job, fool, I told myself, and I could see 'Mmaculata shaking her head, talking to herself.

# 5: THE RING OF CACTUSES

&

When we got back to the stables there were two new men waiting for us: a redheaded Neapolitan and an old man with one eye. "So, where the hell have you two been?" the Boss asked. It was hard to understand their answers, but they said they had narrowly escaped from the police in Enna and then again in Pietraperzia, after which they avoided the towns and crossed the mountains to get here. In all the time with the gang, I never once heard any of them tell a coherent story and these two were no exception. I now think they were incapable of seeing or making sense of what had or was happening to them. In other words, in some way because they couldn't tell their own stories, they kept doing the same thing again and again. Most of us repeat or get stuck in our stories, but they couldn't even tell theirs and the consequences were dire.

Now there was the Boss, the Crazy One, the Basil Man, the three Sicilian brothers from Girgenti, the red-headed Neapolitan, and the one-eyed old man. The gang was growing.

"Get the fire started and let's eat. Where's the wine?" Gino shouted. You could tell the Boss was glad to see the two newcomers. The Crazy One bumped into me, purposely scattering some grain I had in a pot, and said with that crazy smile, "Hey, where do you think you're going?" They were eating outside at a long table under a grapevine next to their usual grill. The fire was lit. Bucolic.

"Who's that kid?" one of the new men asked.

"Nobody, nobody, nobody," whispered the Crazy One, and moved away from me. You never know where help might come from. "Nobody that was, is, or will be," he said to everyone, and crooned it especially to me as he walked back to the table and I walked away to the stables.

I had just finished feeding the animals when I heard the Boss call me to join them. The men sat around the table drinking wine. Smallest was roasting a lamb they had carried away that day. They talked about Santo and what had happened to him. I couldn't make out what they thought. Small raised a toast, "to Generale Santo Caduti Massi, may his soul rest in peace," everyone said, laughing. But the Boss was angry and cut the talk short. Since Santo had disappeared, Gino had been really angry, visibly dejected, but with the money from the merchant, which was much more than they had expected, and the addition of new men, things must have been looking up. That night he got drunk. They were all unusually loud, Gino almost elated.

I was coming from the pit when I heard Artù at the stable. I had been feeling uneasy even before I heard his bellow. The Boss waved me to sit down, and I did, but then I heard Artù again. When I got up, the Boss said, "Where are you going? You did a good job today, Kid, sit down, and have some wine." He was dangerously ebullient. As he passed the jug to me he said to the new men, "This Kid's smart. He would have made somebody a good son." There was a heavy silence. The Crazy One laughed and threw a stone at me. I ducked and grabbed the jug. I didn't hesitate and drank a long swig, but my tongue had a good memory of Pasquale's wine, so I could barely swallow it, but I did. I passed the jug back and just then I heard Artù again.

"I have to take care of something," I said.

"Sit down," Gino said in his low, sullen voice. I sat down. I looked up at the night sky so full of eternity. There was a beautiful gibbous moon sailing and no clouds to mar its light. My eyes were opened. I waited.

We drank until they were out of wine and finally the Basil Man said, "Go get some more, Kid." I went straight to Artù, who was donkey-talking and so agitated he couldn't stand still. The horses were also moving uneasily. I listened carefully but heard nothing unusual. I knew my human ears didn't count. If the animals said they heard something, then something was passing by or standing very still in the dark. If Artù and the horses said it was there, it was there.

"Hey, Kid, where the hell are you?"

"I'm coming." But I waited for a few seconds. Now I could feel it. Someone or something was there. I got another jug of wine and as I walked back to the edge of the camp as quietly as I could, staying in the familiar shadows, I saw something move, something like a bit of brush scuttled by the wind, but there was no wind, and except for that brush everything else was absolutely still. I went back to the table and handed the wine to Smallest, told him I had to close a door, and slipped back to the animals and waited. The donkey and now the horses were stamping. Artù let out another low and long bellow. At the arbor the men were really noisy, really drunk. I was just wondering why no one was at the Boulders on lookout when I heard it—shots, pistol shots, a lot of them. After a few minutes, silence.

I ran back where I could see: there in the lamplight were the Cousin and his sons with guns in their hands, standing looking down at the men, fallen around the table and the fire, most still in their places, moaning or silent. The Neapolitan wasn't moving, Small was doubled over and deadly quiet; the Basil Man was trying to catch his breath, his hand pressing his bloody shirt; the old man with one eye was at the pit looking at his legs and cursing. The remaining two Girgenti brothers had their hands raised.

In the confusion I crept away. I had not seen the Boss or the Crazy One. Where were they? This was not over. I moved to the cover of a large cactus and suddenly I smelled something familiar. Although I couldn't see the Boss, I could smell him. He was a few meters in front of me somewhere, maybe hiding in the ring of cactuses between the small stable and the campsite. Hard as I tried, I couldn't see him, but I did not lose the smell, and then I realized that one of the shadows was wrong: a pointed shape, geometric and peculiar, was tipped beyond the fleshy stems. In the four cactuses, where at night I had often taken sanctuary or hidden, I had never before seen that particular shape. It didn't move. I moved slightly and then I saw it was an elbow. The Boss was crouching, facing the arbor, his back to me, his pistol aimed at the Cousin. Without thinking I sprang at him before he got off his shot. Hanging on to him, I kept him off balance; he wasn't able to shake me, but I wasn't able to break his hold on the pistol. Finally, he shook me loose and turned to face me, but I grabbed his ankle, tipping him backward over into the large cactus thorns, and then jumped clear of him. He let out a low growl, stood up, and, looking me in the eyes, raised his pistol and took aim at my chest.

"I knew it. I knew it would be you. You lucky bastard. Kiss your luck goodbye."

Good God, I thought, it really does happen like this . . . looking me in the eyes, taking his time raising his pistol, like my brothers' penny detective books. He was even smiling.

What happened next I can't completely explain, and since I have only told the Aunt this part of the story, I haven't heard a variety of opinions about it. This is what happened: just as Gino raised his gun, a fierce wind blew up from the earth; heavy cactus limbs and dirt with roots and stones flew around us. Just before he pulled the trigger, I had jumped off to the side, but I must have still been in the line of his fire, because I heard the bullet whizz past my ear. When the wind stopped and the air cleared, I thought I saw a donkey and a figure in a shepherd's cape riding away beyond the cactuses. But I cannot be sure what I saw. The Boss was lying completely still, his pistol resting across the palm of his small open hand. Something had struck him hard. I didn't know if he was dead or alive.

The Cousin and his sons came running. The Boss shook himself, jumped up, and started to run, but in no time they caught him, tied him up like a sausage, and dragged him away. The wind, donkey, and rider were all gone and I sat there stunned. It was to this strange event that I owed my life.

# 6: BITS AND PIECES
# TO PICK UP

လာ

THE COUSIN and his sons left me alone, first nodding
to me and then going about their business. On the
ground, the three wounded men were moaning and
calling out for help. I ran to the stables for blankets and
when I came back one of the Cousin's men was caring
for them as a doctor would. I did what he asked and
soon the bleeding was stopped, but the bandits were
in pieces. The redheaded man was silent and the Basil
Man, first crying and rocking himself, fell into a deep
sleep. The fat flies were getting busy and I swatted them
away from the Basil Man's wound, but you know how
persistent flies are when they're hungry. The buzzing
drove the old man to cursing, only more softly now.
"Close your mouth, you bastard, close your mouth.

Don't touch me," and he closed his eyes. There was a strange, almost ominous calm.

Later, the Cousin and his sons came back and sat down at the campfire with this strange company.

"So we finally meet again," the Cousin said. "What's the matter with your hand?"

"I'm all right," I said. "That bullet just nicked my finger; the bleeding has stopped."

He said no more. I brought some windfalls to the fire; I could see he was waiting for someone. I went back to the stables. Artù was where I'd left him. Within the hour the *carabinieri* came riding into camp. So this was going to be official. After seeing what was left of the gang, the Captain said, "Where's the Kid?"

I walked out. "Here I am," I said, smiling and turning around with one hand in my pocket, the good one over my head, and me going toward them dancing a little tarantella. I was even singing. I stopped suddenly and bowed. I can sometimes be a real fool.

"Well, well, so you're the smart-ass the Mayor's been telling us about. He says you're dangerous—now, is that true?"

"Look at this here, a dangerous murderer," said another of the *carabinieri*.

"The Mayor says you're good with a pistol and we'd better get you," said the Captain with that grin and stupid humor that some people have. All the while he said this he was coming toward me. They were really warming up to it. So the honorable Mayor wanted me dead, too. I had forgotten that I could link that greasy yellow-toothed rat with the gang. After all, I had been his messenger, hadn't I?

"Wait a minute, wait a minute, there's some mistake here," said the Cousin, stepping between us. "There's some mistake here, a big mistake. The boy is one of us. He has been working with us. He's our inside man. Without him, we wouldn't have known where to find these murderers. It was he who told me where they were."

One of the sons spoke up. "In all the confusion just now, we forgot to tell you it was this kid who captured the Boss—with a kitchen knife! How could you know? It was our fault we didn't tell you we were all working together. If it wasn't for him, we wouldn't have found them. Yes, yes, we call him the inside man."

Wow! What diplomats. I was impressed.

"He used to be a little snot-nosed kid, but he's no *muccarusu* anymore," added Pasquale's cousin, putting an arm around me and pulling me toward them.

"That's true," his boys said, making a place for me.

"There are questions to be answered," the Captain persisted, looking at me. "We hear there was a woman with them; where is she?"

"A woman?" I said, "Imagine a woman! No one ever talked about a woman. What would a woman be doing here?"

The bandits were taken away by the *carabinieri* and we waited until dawn to leave. We were the Cousin, his sons, two others and me.

I found out the man who had helped the wounded really was a doctor, son of the good Dr. Serafini who was killed by the bandits after curing one of them. "In the end my revenge was just to be like my father, God rest his good soul. But with a luckier outcome, if possible. Now I can go back home in peace."

When they were sitting quietly for a while I asked the Cousin, "How did you know where to find us?"

"You told me."

"I told you? When?"

"When I saw you in town that time."

"What did I tell you?"

" 'Donkey Shit,' that's what you said."

"It must be a coincidence. I never heard of a place anywhere with that name."

"No, that's right, but when you said 'donkey shit' I remembered 'Donkey Shit's Place,' and I knew right away it was where they were hiding. Donkey Shit's Place, is just what we used to call this farm. You know what's funny? The nickname has nothing to do with donkeys. It has to do with the owner, a man who was so greedy that we called him Donkey Shit. When the typhus came, we asked for our pay so we could leave while we were still able, and he said, 'I'll collect the rents later and pay you,' but he never did. Soon, on top of being hungry, we became sick, but that hard-hearted bastard said, 'What are they complaining about? They have plenty of prickly pears. Do they want doctors, too?' We were so sick of prickly pears my poor mother turned her head away at the sight of a little piece my father offered her in the palm of his hand. Later, we heard that the great villa had completely burned down. This building where the bandits slept was the overseer's house. Over there are the French stables, built a hundred years ago for his grandfather's Arabians. After the typhus we never came back, and as far as anyone knew there was nothing left here. We had sent someone a while ago to check it out, but he came back saying no one was here and we believed him. I thought I might not remember how to get back myself, but that isn't true. Once I got close I remembered, all right, I remembered everything."

"So hearing that name was just luck?"

"Luck? Yes, I guess. Do you like to gamble at cards?"

"At my house we always played between Christmas and New Year's. We really liked Briscola."

"Well, if you like playing cards, you know that luck doesn't belong to anyone and yet there are things you can do to get luck to sit down next to you. Without even stopping to think about it you know two things after the hand is dealt: the numbers, so you understand the real possibilities in everybody's hand and what is likely; and the feeling in your bones, which tells you how the cards are falling, not a wish only, but a feel for how they are falling for yourself and others. Neither of these, of course, is infallible. I don't know, my boy, what luck really is, and if I knew I wouldn't want to say it out loud."

"And what about you?" I asked.

"Oh! I love playing cards, but I have no special luck with them. I've only learned to work hard, that's what has been given to me and my good callused hands," he said seriously. "Learning to do something really well is the only thing I have. I try to be smart and play a good game of cards, but that's all."

"I'd say the same as you about hard work. But, you know, you all did have luck. There's usually a man at the lookout up there. If he had been there, you would have been in serious trouble. He just wasn't there tonight. Wasn't that luck?"

"I bet they had that man above the Cat Boulders, am I right? That would be the obvious place."

"Yes, that's where. The Cat Boulders."

"Ah! But we never would have come that way. No, not

by way of the Cat Boulders. I know this place well enough to know that would be the lookout. I took us by a detour, behind the stables. No, son, that wasn't luck. But I'd say in all of this it was you who had luck."

"I'd say, sir, that you and maybe someone else came to help me."

"And who was that?"

"I don't know for sure," I said.

When we went back to the farmhouse there was not a single sign of Immaculata anywhere. (I didn't dare call out her name.) Not one thing of hers was left, not even the burnt candles or the picture of Saint Agatha.

When the Cousin left me off in my town's square, he picked up the sack Immaculata had given me for my belongings.

"Well, well, *talìa, talìa,* look, look," he said, handing it down to me. "For a young man you've got a lot of stuff already."

"Only junk," I said, pulling out a large jacket, and a whole lot of embarrassing kid stuff fell out with it: some forks that I had carved, a handful of dried chestnuts, and an old kitchen knife. "Just junk," I said. But I stopped short of something heavy which sat at the bottom of the sack, something I hadn't put in. It was a very heavy goat-skin bag tied with thin string. It was really heavy, like silver or gold. Now I knew why the cousin said I had stuff. It was tied with that old asparagus thread of 'Mmaculata's. She was something, all right.

"Put it back, put it all back, before you make people envious of you." He laughed nicely. "And besides that, you'll be sharing something else with us." He winked and rode off.

And that was true: I was given a share of the reward, and it was quite a bit of money. They brought Artù and Pasquale's cart with the casks back to his family. The family gave me Artù. (He and his friend are in the pasture right now.) The Basil Man, the redheaded Neapolitan, Small, and the old man were taken out of a prison hospital. Santo had already melted into air, so the Boss, the two youngest Girgenti brothers, and the old man with one eye all went to trial. The Crazy One was never found. The police were hot to find 'Mmaculata, but she never turned up.

'Mmaculata used to say, "I know, Kid, you've never seen Gino try to be convincing except with a gun, but I've seen him charm people, close up convince them of anything. He could take this one miserable big lie and tell it to ten different people in ten different ways as if it was all true. If they didn't believe him he'd get crazy mad, but if they did believe him he'd have contempt. In the end he did whatever he wanted to them anyway. He doesn't know a lie from the truth. There's no one inside him who knows the truth or any way to it anymore. I think he's convinced while he's telling the lie, but when it's over he's crazier than before. He's a certain kind of crazy, but I don't know what you'd call it."

The bandits had a six-week trial in Palermo. They were defended by three of the most able lawyers. I saved all the accounts written by a famous Sicilian journalist who spent every day of those six weeks in the courtroom. Her works are compared favorably to the articles written about bandits on the border between England and Scotland in the same year. You can read it for yourself in *The Chronicles of Palermo*, volume six, number III, pp. 25–87.

The bandits implicated the Mayor, who was also tried, but he got off on technicalities. Technicalities, my foot. I still see him in our town; he's an old decrepit man, who sits alone in the square spitting tobacco juice into a little pot he carries. Everyone laughs, but I don't. Because of him there was a bit of reform in our town and the next mayor was an honest ex-soldier. He was in only for one term.

At the trial, the Boss pleaded not guilty to thirty-two counts of manslaughter. Not guilty, to thirty-two deaths! He claimed he was himself a victim of a chain of circumstances that he had no control over. He said he had been born of honest parents, and had himself been an honest man up until the age of twenty-five. He had a wife and children, and it was family troubles that first prompted him to kill his brother-in-law. He feared the man's family would retaliate, so he ran off and gave himself over to the countryside, admitting from then on he was a highway-man and could never go back to society.

"Did you kill Pasquale Di Stefano?" asked the prosecutor.

"It wasn't my fault. It wasn't me."

"Who killed Dr. Giovanni Serafini?"

"It wasn't my fault. It wasn't me."

In the end he was sent to jail for life.

In this world, where so much human evil goes around as though it were ordinary and lies are told with no shame attached, it's a miracle when good souls catch a break. It is often said "Be careful of people who have no shame." They can kill your friend or take over an entire country and kill its compassion. Disaster is everywhere these days.

When I went back home, my parents cried for a week. I didn't return to school, but went instead to work for the blacksmith. The times were better and for the moment hunger was routed. Everybody in town was eating again. I even worked in the blacksmith's kitchen cooking for pay on the last Friday of every month, which is the day of the horse fair in our town.

As I said, I was given my share of the reward money. That money made everyone happy: my family, Pasquale's family, and all our neighbors who had been down on their luck. "You really did bring home the Golden Bells from the Ogres," they said. I don't know about that, but I did share all the money, and finally I gave the last of it for the Feast of St. Joseph. So for a while everyone in town thought of me as the kid in the story of "Tridicinu," who went to the Ogres' house and brought the Golden Bells back to town. The old story says that if you go to the place no one else would dare go, and if you make it back, then you bring something that was missing.

Someone asked me what happened to me and my brothers. Although they were glad to see me again and were friendly enough, I could feel they were afraid of me, maybe of what I had gone through, maybe what I now knew. They stayed away from me. We were never as close as we had been as children. It was true that I was different.

I had been lucky to find 'Mmaculata. She was a special kind of grandmother from the old tales. Not a fairy Godmother, no, no, not that kind, but one who knows how to battle demons. In the story a kid comes to get the golden hairs from her grandson's head (he's a giant or sometimes an ogre) and asks her for help. She recognizes this kid and says, "Yes." What she recognizes is what makes the other half of the luck.

In life it's close but different. She is a real grand-mother who picks the kid up from the street, or maybe the kid knocks on her door. Basically she is not going to let that kid get away with much: *Tuck in your shirt. Wash your hands. Brush your jacket.* But if everyone else is hard, then she can be the opposite. She gives you some-thing good to eat, a place to sleep. No matter what else happens, you know she loves you and would protect you with her last breath. She doesn't allow stealing or mis-ery, and she doesn't allow you to feel pathetic. *Don't lis-ten to people who call you names; they don't know who we are. Some people tell lies, so you're going to have to judge for yourself who to listen to and who to ignore. You have a brain, use it. You have a good heart, use it. Courage, my child, courage!* And so on and so on. She's anywhere and everywhere. I know you could add your own list here. Thank God for the tough Old Ones who know the per-ilous, narrow path. After all, it was made by their own footsteps. Lucky me, who found such an old woman in a den of thieves and murderers, but then where else would I have found her?

We say in Sicilian, *"La tu casa, Ti stringi e ti basa,"* your own house hugs and kisses you." This we truly believe. Although I visit my mother and father often, I have a new home here at the Inn and in the flat fields and mountains. I tell people that the only regret I have is that I never again saw 'Mmaculata, but then neither did the *carabinieri,* who until a few years ago were still looking for her. Even though the Cousin called me the "inside man," that person was really 'Mmaculata. She certainly got Santo to quit, and who knows who else she helped besides me. I can't help thinking about what happened at the ring of cactuses with the Boss. Who was the rider who saved me?

"Being natural and awake like a child or a creature. That's one of the places luck comes from," says the Aunt. "Being innocent or just plain truthful."

Although I no longer openly mourn for Pasquale as I did in those days, I have never gotten over his death as people said I would. I still miss my friend, more than miss him. Who can take another's place? When you lose someone you've truly loved, you never forget them, but you learn to put your jacket over the misery and get on with it. And all those well-meaning people who told me that I would get over it, I know now they didn't know what they were saying or had not yet lost anyone they really loved. Yes, it's true that no one can exactly take another's place, and this alone left a hole in my life, a place where I fell through to memory and story. A great poet said that we make all art from memory and hope. Memory is a funny companion. I myself love and trust it. And hope? It is stranger still. Both qualities are essential in my everyday life, as essential as seeing that thin red bird that stitches the high branches of a fir tree with its flight.

Sometimes I go to play cards at a farm house down in the valley and I think of the Cousin's talk about cards and luck. One tells you that luck is in the cards and in the probabilities of numbers and the other says that luck is in you. I can't deny both. The possibilities begin simply with the probability of the draw, but then if the element of choice is introduced the whole thing changes wildly. The question of choice and chance. As soon as you are given the possibility, the chance of replacing cards, of having more choices, a whole new and more complicated set of numbers comes into play. A game where you can get your cards replaced even once gives you enormous possibilities compared to a game where you must play only what you have been dealt.

The other night the Aunt and I were sitting over a good plate of chickpeas and *ditali,* talking about what happened to me and those bandits twenty years ago.

"With all my practice standing, stooping, hiding in unexpected places, making myself invisible," I said, "when the moment really came, I didn't save myself; I ended up not doing anything at all."

"Oh! I wouldn't say you did nothing. It all counts somehow."

"Maybe it was a miracle."

"Then again, maybe not. Maybe it was some idiot who was lost, got mixed up there by mistake, and was on his or her way home, and you were just lucky."

"Or maybe it was someone who knew exactly what she or he was doing and I'd still think it was a miracle. Besides," I said, "what part do you think luck plays in miracles?"

"Ah! A modernist," she said with a laugh. "No, no, luck is still of this ordinary life, on its crest, maybe. Luck happens for the sake of our story, not really for individual humans, who think they are more than they are. What happened to you might have been grace and a good deed coming together. I hear there are entire commissions who pass on the validity of miracles. My grandmother used to be the expert on them in our village. 'They do not come from oddities in this world but from God's will,' she used to say. 'Miracles are miracles because they happen at the edges, outside our plans or purposes, inside the seam where all things meet.' Well, Carù, who knows? Maybe it was a miracle."

"Have you ever experienced one?"

"I only know a story about the breath of a donkey

on a freezing night. It saved a sick child's life," she said. "When the dying child opened her eyes and felt that beautiful creature's breath on her neck, she felt she was going to live. I still think of that as a miracle."

It's the end of the century and like pins despair is on everyone's seat, especially for the young people around here. *Miseria* has come around again and there is much suffering. Hunger is hunger but *miseria* means starvation. In these years people all over the Island pack up and leave.

"Thank God no person or creature goes away from our Inn hungry," says the Aunt.

The Greeks used to call Sicily "Ceres' wheat basket." But we have trouble even in what was our excess. Our own markets have become flooded with imported wheat. It has made this a bad year for our poor farmers. Food has again become a commodity, so much more "stuff" to make into money. How can food be a commodity? Isn't it life itself? What reasoning is this? We feel awe at the sight of fields of wheat and encourage another turn of fate's wheel so that we can feel that once again.

I wish I could give you the balance that exists in the old stories, that would make it a social blunder to say the word "commodity" without first adding an adjective like "gentle," or "supple," or "fleeting," or "sacred."

When I read what you have just read to the Aunt, she

said, "I myself like a story where donkeys and fava beans are mentioned. And if you could include beings that come in numbers like mice and flies, I'd like that, too."

"Mice and flies?"

"Why not? You have something against them?"

"No, all right, I'll put in mice and flies."

Yesterday, the Aunt came shuffling into the kitchen with the question that is forever on her lips: "When are you going to marry, Joseph? You're an old thirty. No woman is going to have you if you don't propose."

"How can I ask anyone to live here?" I answer, teasing. "We don't have all the goods of the cities."

"Yeah, yeah." She laughs and shakes her head. "Our place here is better than the new hotel that opened on the main road. The Wild Boar. There hasn't been a boar around there in fifty years, except for the owner."

"Find someone who knows, or wants, or already cherishes this place. Or simply look nearby for the right woman, ask her to marry and then go live with her family. It will be what she wants anyway. And what about Elizabetta? Do you think she would consider coming back to the mountains?"

"I paid a visit to her and her family when I went to Palermo last month."

"That's good, that's good. It's a start." The Aunt looks at me and says, "Hurry up, Giuseppuzzu. My legs hurt and my eyes are dimming, poor Saint Anna is tired of listening to me, and every day I light candles to Sant' Agatuzza for you. I want to meet your sweetheart, sooner rather than later."

It's my turn to smile. "You never know, Zia; you never know."

"That's true," she says, "but don't become silent or clumsy. Women want to hear a good word or even a song. You have a nice voice. They will like that. Share what you have."

What do I have? My working hands, strong heart, and the place that I know. This place has shown us a great deal and given everything it has (it cannot help it). We have given back all we have (we cannot help it). There is enough new in the air to keep us alive, so we choose to add some of the old ways that have not been improved upon yet. I have waited patiently, but like the sirocco I, too, am a creature of what happens. At the end of winter, the storytelling almost over, there is a quiet expectation before the cultivating begins.

A week ago I felt wild asparagus about to appear. The Aunt says the best ones are already out.

"Sew the hanging buttons onto your jacket, Giuseppe. No one is going to take your courting seriously unless you take it seriously. Brush your coat well. Move yourself."

*Dearest Bettina,*

*It is late. Today was a strange day, no, not strange, but special. Last night while we slept, the sirocco blew. This morning we awoke to red sand over everything. The wind says, Africa? Sicily? I don't know that kind of border. A sea apart? What does it matter? A shift and something happens. Everything is close today. "Here, there," it says,"what is that to me? Here, there, where? This is what is. Know it or not, that's up to you." The time is now. It's the wind that decided last night, not humans.*

*In your last letter you wrote that you longed to come home and your brothers said the same. Yes, dear One, come home. You said once you knew, were absolutely certain that we would walk again up into these mountain fields to find wild asparagus together. When? Is this the time? I write now that it would give me joy if you all would allow me to help in this move back home. Please, remember I can do anything and everything—all that needs to be done. Love asks and love answers. Love commands and love obeys.*

*Affectionately yours,*
*Joseph*

*As I write this, someone is knocking. Who could it be at this late hour?*

6.1.
845-679-8189
g.t@netstep.net